The First Martian Murder

by

Trevor Palmer

Foreword and acknowledgements

This story is fiction and the views expressed by the characters in it are not intended to reflect the opinions of the author in any way.

In researching the fast-moving technology featured herein, the author was frequently overawed by the sheer belief and enthusiasm of those scientists, technicians and associated staff and support who have pushed us so close to making another giant step for mankind – this time in red sand! So, my tribute here is to everyone at NASA and SpaceX.

Credit for the cover background photo ... NASA/JPL-Caltech/MSSS

Copyright © 2018 Trevor Palmer

All rights reserved

ISBN – 10: 1720841683

ISBN – 13: 978-1720841685

The First Martian Murder

☼

I was furious. Steaming! And yet the cause was now a week into history. It was no use reviewing it all over again yet I seemed unable to stop doing just that - I had spent a week of lying in bed each night, tired but with the damn thing still buzzing around in my brain. Therefore, no sleep until 2-ish. It was just impossible: insanely impossible.

And so, back yet again one week to when it started - which meant I now had only one more week to go …

Back to that call into the boss's office, the boss being a bean-counter. A self-opinionated prick in my opinion. As par for the course, a boss who knew all about spread-sheets, monthly projections, etc. Nothing about AI robots or *the men who built them or programmed them*! But here I was, in the hardwood chair he'd waved me into while he sprawled with all the timeless ease in the world in his soft leather one.

"Hi, Dave. How's Project Intel-5 going?"

The invite - no, command - to go up to his office was surprising enough but, for him to actually carry the talk into work - and my work not his - had me sitting upright. I passed on saying a short 'Well, pretty good, thanks.' and decided to be sort of relaxed and, mmh, kind of chatty. See where this was going …

"Pretty good, thanks." This still seemed a good starter, whatever. "Now we've fitted the improved Explore Ex10 circuitry it's getting somewhere. The next ste …"

"Good. Good." My expansive, chatty style hadn't got me far. "Your new assistant, Goodwin; Colin Goodwin isn't it? How's he coming along. Pretty capable would you say?"

"Er, yes. I would say so. Clever bloke and has picked up things on the Intel-5 project quite quickly." My brain was spinning. Was this all about Col? Or me? Staffing probs maybe? Oh, stop trying to second guess, he'll come out with it when he's good and ready. But, that wasn't my style …

"What's this all about, Chief?" I knew he didn't like that title but I wasn't into 'sirs'. He wasn't a bloody knight. He often said to me and others, 'Call me Walter'. Some of us had thought something similar suited but we didn't say it aloud.

He paused and tried chewing a pencil tip. I wondered where he got these pencils from which seemed to give him a little boost.

"Ever thought of yourself as an astronaut?" Now he had my attention - but not my comprehension. He'd stopped chewing his booster and his pale blue eyes had taken on an unusual gleam. It wasn't quite amusement, though that was there. It wasn't steely, so this wasn't about getting the heave-ho. Nothing to do but wait. For some reason I shrugged and spread my arms out. Now he explained …

"This company is not only funded by the UN, or dis-united Nations as I know you like to call them, but, in reality it is run by them. If they say, 'Make us a robot to do what-ever', we make them a robot to do what-ever. There is no argument. Once upon a time there may have been but that time is long gone. Now, believe me or not, they have said 'We want your top AI engineer to go to Mars.' He paused to let a non-bean-counter slowly add up where this was going. Ten seconds after straight away I got there. I had dismissed the idea of him seeking my approval of Col as the likely astronaut. This was all about me. The sign that I had worked this out must have been the way my jaw dropped. Now I looked for the joke and put that thought into words …

"Walter!" - good heavens, he must have scored a hit - "If this was April Fool's day …" But since it wasn't. What sort of twisted humour had he embarked on? He'd never shown this side of his nature before … "If you are telling me what I think you're telling me … that the UN want me to go to Mars? It's totally ridiculous. Apart from the fact that I can't think of a single reason why I should, it's impossible. For one thing, I'm not trained in any way for it. I 've not been in the Air Force, never flown a plane although, like ten million others, I've been on holiday in a jet. That's all. On top of which … am I fit enough? As far as I know, I'm not too bad for a 35-year-old. No hardening arteries that I know of. But it's crazy. So, what's the trick? Some sort of team-building course? I've done my share of those."

His eyes didn't change as they held mine. "Plenty of people are making space flights now. The space-flight terminal in New Mexico is doing good business, so I understand. I'm surprised there are enough people with all that spare money. Anyway, they aren't all super fit, they just have the wealth." Here he gave a slight chuckle. "And now you can match them … you have all the UN's trillions to buy your ticket."

I was speechless for a while; a rarity.

At last I plodded on. "But these super-rich remain in orbit. I don't know how long for. But a trip to Mars takes months. And then, how long will I be there for? Then more months to return. What's that add up? A couple of years? And, back to my first point … what on Earth for?" I realised that was maybe the wrong metaphor and gave a slight smile.

Now it was my boss's turn to shrug and hold his arms wide. "This, er, talk, is just to forewarn you. They didn't apprise me of any facts at all but they are sending a couple of reps tomorrow to explain … just to you, I might add … and to get your agreement. But, and here I should warn you. You *will give your agreement.* Let us make no bones about it. They have unlimited power and they can be quite ruthless so, if they say, 'You're going to Mars, Mr Harper' you *will* be going to Mars."

This was the point where my anger started to build. Well, no-one likes to be coerced. Coerced and kept in the dark. And the recent signing-on of Col, a suitable deputy. This wasn't sudden planning. Worst of all … leaving my girlfriend Sue behind for maybe 2 years. For what? I had a good life now. Good sex. Pleasant company. With a good future maybe, both in and out of the workplace. All to be put in the dustbin or at best put on hold for a long period of my life. And, running it all around in my mind even while sitting in the chief's office was the conclusion that it must be to do with my work here - to do with Artificial Intelligence.

··········

"Dave. Small meetings room. They're here."

"Thanks, Col." I'd given him some of the gen so he didn't need any explanation of why my face looked like that of one of our androids – all tight and expressionless.

"You goin' to tell them to stuff it?"

I shrugged into my jacket and slung the short, white coat which was my uniform onto the bench. "Can't do that, my old chum. But I'm not a happy bunny I can tell you. Still … You should be happy. Almost instant promotion. At least I know you can take care of things while I'm gone."

Colin gave a leery smirk. "Does that include Susan?"

I put a false note of warning into my reply. "You better behave yourself there. No telling what subtle mods I've sneaked into Intel-5's circuitry. He'll be keeping a beady eye on you while I'm gone. And, talking about being gone … I'm gone now. Cheers."

Col gave a limp wave and turned away while I headed for the lift and the third floor.

I tapped on the meetings room door and entered. Two well-dressed individuals looked up at me, making a prelim assessment. They'd already placed their brief cases on the table, opened them up and strewn an assortment of papers in front of them. One was a big man, middle-aged with side hair going grey. Eyes that wore a bland, neutral look but had a deeper, harder light in them. Odd eyes. Unreadable. But he only earned a quick glance. It was his companion who had more of my attention. The other UN rep was a youngish woman, mid-thirties maybe but I'm not good at that guessing game. Her glasses had heavy but trendy frames that failed to conceal her natural good looks. She filled out her lightweight jacket in the way that most men liked too. I belonged in that number and, quite unbidden, the thought came into my mind that maybe, yes, just maybe, she would also be coming along on the trip to Mars.

She waved a hand at me indicating a chair placed opposite to them. Of course I ignored that, strolled across behind them and took a glance at their papers. The perfume from lady UN rep made it doubly worth the deviation. They made no attempt at covering up any of the papers so I strolled on past them and casually proceeded to pour myself a coffee from the tray of goodies on a sideboard. It's always a better class of brew than ours at the sharp end of production. I twisted round and raised an eyebrow - I always liked to practice that.

"Anyone else for a cuppa?"

They both shook their heads as though they were wired together. Ah, UN reps. All business.

I chose a seat, more or less where the girl had indicated. My assumed suavity was spoiled slightly by my rattling cup and saucer as I sat down. Well, I was used to a mug. Never-the-less, I gave them the 'both eyebrows raised' look and spread my hands out which is unlearned sign-language for 'Carry on then. Explain all.'

I was surprised when the lady spoke first. It wasn't that the female sex wasn't now fully integrated in all sorts of business matters but I somehow had assumed that age still carried that extra bit of weight.

"Mr Harper ... I'm Anna and this is my colleague, Rob. You know we're from the UN. You know we would like you to go to Mars. And that's about all you do know. It must seem so, er, outlandish ..." she gave a slight smile and, oh, I did like those lips. "What can I possibly be required to do on Mars, you're puzzlin'. Or even on the journey there. So, we're here to tell you and answer any questions that are answerable. Shall I begin?"

"Sure. Fire away. But ... I already know what it's all about."

For the first time - admittedly in the very short space of time I'd had to assess her, but it somehow seemed longer - she looked thrown out of her stride. Greying hair by her side didn't look, well, anything. Instead, he said in a short, clipped tone, "He's lying."

"Oh, no, I'm not." I retorted, bringing in a note of indignation. "It's well known in the artificial intelligence industry that my favourite chocolate bar, one that's survived for many, many years, has been discovered while searching for underground water reserves on Mars. I'm required to go there and do a practical analysis to see whether or not it's worthwhile mining the stuff ..."

UN lady relaxed and showed very white teeth between the highly desirable lips. Greying hair said nothing and just stared ahead. Ah, well; everyone can't have a sense of humour. Hey, I thought. What am I doing with a childish attempt at it? It's cool, hard facts I need. I twisted my face into a kind of apology and opened up the palm of one hand which was, of course, more sign language for 'Sorry! Carry on, please.'

Anna nodded. She took a deep breath. "The United Nations has many aspects of its work. One of these, not usually written about or spoken of in the media, is to do with international law applied to neutral territories. Our department is about inter-state law activation modules."

"Islam," I said softly, almost to myself.

Anna nodded and smiled gently and ruefully. "Yes. Believe it or not, this was quite unintentional. We get so many chiefs blurting out new acronyms and if those chiefs are powerful enough, we're stuck with'em. But, forget any connection. It doesn't exist."

"So, what's this new ISLAM all about then?"

"Mars, like certain very cold regions of Earth were years ago, has been declared Neutral Territory. That's a recent designation but you may have heard of it. It means that under UN law ..."

"Is there such a thing?" I butted in.

"Oh, yes. There certainly is. And under that law's jurisdiction, no country or limited alliance of countries may seek to rule or to develop the land wherein it holds sway."

"Pity the native Americans didn't know about it years ago," I couldn't help muttering.

Anna nodded. "We're a little late but we are trying to get there. Thus, Mars is a designated neutral territory. Its wealth will be shared equally - well, proportionately," she amended. "But it's the application of laws that can present problems."

I breathed out slowly and looked down mournfully into my now empty cup. "I still don't see where I'm going to fit into this picture," I said and added quietly, "And why it will take 2 years out of my life to do the fitting in." I stood up. It was no use; I had to refill my cup.

When I was re-seated, Anna had somehow become fully braced to get down to the nitty gritty. She pulled a serious look from somewhere - UN training? - and began …

"We've had an incident on Mars. With one of the two teams which are currently working there. We believe a murder in fact may have been committed." She paused to let this sink in. When I made no comment - I was too flabbergasted - she rolled on. "So, the UN is sending a team to examine the evidence: murder or just an accident. If murder - or not, come to that - to then determine if there is a guilty party. When that's been settled, take appropriate action. There!"

I thought for a moment. "No, not 'there'. You've not plugged me into this game yet. Having read a couple of Sherlock Holmes books or Harry Bosch, come to that, doesn't qualify me as a super-sleuth. I just fail to …"

Anna used both hands, palms down, to make gentle pushing motions. More sign language for 'Calm down. I'm coming to that now.' "We already have a super-sleuth booked for the trip, Dave." She hesitated fractionally before delivering the big one … "You will simply be there to look after him. Make sure he functions at his very best." Now she crossed her arms and, my bet was, ticked off the seconds 'til the penny dropped.

Ten seconds after straight away, it hit me. "Your super-sleuth is a robot! Any circuit malfunction, Dave reaches for his screwdriver."

"Not a screwdriver, if you please."

I looked, completely stunned, from Anna to her companion, speaking for only the second time. Rob ... Robin ... Robot Intelligence. I'd been totally sand-bagged.

....

✿ ✿

The week leading up to my departure for Mars was about as mixed a bag of mind-blowing incidents as could be thrown at any one individual. First and foremost, of course, was my session - for want of better terminology - with Sue.

Cleverly waiting for our sex to start winding down before I revealed all ... well, you know what I mean: the Mars thing not my magnificent body ... she was, by stages, unbelieving, in shock, suspicious (was this just a ruse on my part), thoughtful - and with the questions which go with that, etc. Then, reaching a conclusion, which at first produced a flood of tears but resolved into the practicalities and truth which only a woman can come up with. Finally, a bleak, thousand-yard stare into the future - or lack of it.

Of course, I was hugely affected by all this. I'm a lot more emotional and caring than I show to most other people. It ended with an agreed assessment. Our relationship would not survive 2 years - or more? - apart. There would be no promises of good intentions and, certainly, no quick marriage. We would have to do what most other people do - play the cards of life as they are dealt to us. I guessed she was, like me though: not very enamoured by the miserably small pile of chips in front of me.

What more can I say about this episode? Quite simply, we were finished.

....

I was still partially numbed by the time spent with Sue and assumed that a general briefing about Mars, the journey there, and what then, would be something I could absorb without having to think too deeply. After all, being reasonably interested in space - what was out there and what explorations were in process - I doubted there wasn't too much more for me to learn at this stage. The details of the flight being the exception certainly. But this next step was simply a first meeting. With those UN personnel in the know. The artists just doing a few rough brush strokes for a student.

Thus, early in the final week I was invited (summoned) to a meeting in London. Why everything of any significance still had to take place in the capital city, I don't know. Attempts had supposedly been made by the UK government to 'recognise' Manchester, Birmingham and a few other contenders as places of importance but we all seemed to head towards London and its horrendous traffic jams when it came to it.

A taxi finally saw me to the right building. It looked as though it had a government connection (don't they all?) but the polished brass by the door said 'United Nations – Inter-state Department'. I smiled; no ISLAM then.

When I had satisfied complicated security systems and their attendant guards and stern-looking staff (why can't security people ever smile?), I was led, still caressing my new identitag, to a room whose ceiling was further away than the end of the room. Robin the robot sleuth wasn't there and, disappointingly, neither was Anna. The new team tasked with briefing me was 3-strong ... a fairly old character with a very wrinkled face but who looked vaguely familiar: a guy of about my own age, tanned and fit-looking, sprawling nonchalantly in his seat: lastly, a bespectacled young fellow in a slick, dark suit, upright and alert. The old guy was on the right, facing me as I flopped into a chair, with the other two completing a trio in age order.

This time age did seem to count - it was the old guy who took command ...

With a friendly nod but no handshake, he said, "Glad to meet you, Dave." Nodding at the others, he introduced them, "Rick Templar, who'll be your pilot and Denton Allgood, our own AI expert specialising on Mars robotics. You may have seen my picture in the media a few times - just James or Jim will do. Have been into space a few times but pleased to be now retired. We're here to fill in your lack of knowledge about this mission and we are going to assume, perhaps quite wrongly, that you know squat - a space term," he grinned, "for sod all or nothing."

I nodded and smiled back. "Pretty accurate," I agreed.

"Tell us how you picture Mars," he asked.

I summoned up mental pictures and my limited knowledge.

"A long, long way away," I began, refraining from bringing in the time factor even though that still niggled. "Very cold and inhospitable. Air unbreathable. Red dust and rocks. Windy. The sort of place to stay in your cosy camp structure, whatever that may be. If you have to go out, it's in a space suit - and you can then jump about like a spring lamb because of the low gravity, though not quite as high off the ground as on the moon. I don't know how we eat or communicate. I guess that's the essence of what I know. Not much, is it?"

Just James gave a gentle smile again. "It isn't that you know little - it's that some of what you know has, mmh, changed. Things have moved on a bit in the last ten years. Take your jumping around ... I've done that on the moon but it isn't a technique for Mars. We walk about there. You're right about it being a long, long way but, there again, we've brought it closer - in effect."

"A gravity machine!" I joked.

"No. A damn faster drive than rockets. Still use the old transfer orbits - slingshot effect, to you - so, the distance hasn't changed. But, by God, we've got some poke in our engines now."

This was something new to me.

"Some sort of plasma thing?" I tried, plucking something scientific-sounding out of the depths of my knowledge.

James Whoever-he-was managed a tolerant smile. "It's electromagnetic propulsion drive, Em-Drive for short," he explained. "The power source is nuclear - no more fuel containers, no more jets of searing flames slamming down onto concrete lift-off pads. No more worrying about leaky seals and becoming toast before you're even past the first clouds …"

"Well, if we're riding out on a nuclear power plant, I can think of a few other worries to take the place of those you've eliminated," I said. Then, as I began to roll this new super-drive around in my head - "And what about all this speed? - not to mention acceleration. I have quite a delicate flesh-and-blood body. I wasn't built on Krypton, you know."

James nodded but it was our pilot, Rick Templar, who spoke now for the first time. He had a deep, growly voice.

"You'd be surprised just how fast men can go. The acceleration, we take care of by making it uniform. A steady build up. A sudden blast from zero to maximum g and, yes, that would be pretty, er, calamitous. Even a g-suit wouldn't work then."

Now, even Denton Allgood, perhaps trying to live up to his name, chipped in. "Don't worry about the technicalities of the space flight, Dave. We'll take good care of you."

I'd been pretty angry many times over the preceding days and now I couldn't help it spilling over. I stared with no attempt to hide my fury into the baby eyes behind the thick lenses. A virtual child, who was probably closeted every day in a pleasant workshop or office with his robots, was now trying to lecture me in safety aspects of riding on a 100-Megawatt nuclear bomb.

"*We'll* take good care of me, will *we*? ..." I was about to add more but Templar cut in.

"Dave!" It was a warning shot. "Denton here may have been given a rather short intro as an AI robotics expert but he also designed the control systems for the propulsion unit and - remember this - he has *personally* taken part in the field trials of that and not from any safe observation structure either." H paused to let this sink in. "I reckon few people are better qualified to say they'll take good care of somebody."

My anger balloon deflated rather rapidly then. A shrug and a 'sorry' aimed at the young wizard was all I could manage.

Perhaps to make sure I had cooled off, the rest of the meeting was adjourned until the afternoon. We hadn't covered much, I thought.

....

The afternoon weather was slowly deteriorating, light cloud increasing to darker rain-threatening cover. Like most places, London was not at its best when this happened so, I wasn't too unhappy to be spending the next few hours indoors.

We had split up for lunch. I managed to find a small, homely café that wasn't crowded and I enjoyed a pasta salad mix that tasted OK and I ate slowly so that I could think about things. Accompanying the thinking, I slowly dragged up a few questions which I noted down on a small pad I'd brought with me ...
1. Who else was making the trip - and for each one, for what purpose?
2. More detail about the flight - where from, what to wear and what luggage?
3. What to do in flight?
4. Who was already on Mars and what were they up to?
5 - and last for the time being - I couldn't just sit around waiting for Robin to malfunction so, what was I supposed to do when we got there?
Oh, and 6, - after I signalled the waitress - What was the evidence for murder and, from that thought, any possibility of me becoming another victim?

....

We resumed at almost 2.00. Same room, same people but, for some reason, we all seem to have decided on a slightly different seating arrangement. Young Denton had moved farther away from me but he needn't have worried - my anger was spent and I even felt quite contrite. Maybe that was the pasta.

I placed my little notebook in plain view and James Sutheridge - I'd now recalled his name and some of his exploits in space - nodded at it and spread his hands out.

"Shoot," he invited.

"I know three people - well two and a bot - who'll be making the trip. I guess there may be others ...?" I left it hanging for the reply.

James nodded. "There will be, you're right there. One will be another bot. He or it will be pre-programmed for soil analysis in particular. That's because we want to leave him behind to help the team investigating the Martian surface. More correctly, what's under the surface. But its capabilities extend to tissue analysis too. Tissue includes blood, skin, clothing, whatever."

"So, initially, it'll be like a forensic scientist assisting with the, er, death?" I clarified.

"That's about it. This 'him', 'it' thing, by the way - We've already got a name for him." He smiled his little, quirky smile again. "Sandman," he said.

I leaned back, joining in the smiles. "Will I be looking after Sandman as well as Robin, then?" I queried.

Now young Denton joined in. He'd decided he was on safe ground but was also eager to cement a better relationship between us all ...

"No. The UN department which planned this whole thing had you pegged for Robin because of your, um, expertise in that area ..." He paused, sensing that I would want to clarify something here. He was right.

I said, "Right from the start, I've wondered 'why me?' Why wasn't Robin's creator - or someone from his development team or at least from the company that manufactured him - the better choice to make this trip?" I spread my hands and contrived to look suitably puzzled.

The eyes behind the thick lenses blinked. He nodded. "I can see why you would wonder about that but here's what other UN sources have told us - First and foremost, the original creator of Robin has passed on ..." I always liked that gentle way of saying someone was dead. Not so blunt … "and his closest colleague is, not to put too fine a point on it, a bit over the hill for sitting, as you put it, on a 100-Megawatt nuclear drive." He waited for all of 5 seconds, just in case. "Now, your own record, your resume, …" I wondered at a possible American connection "…followed the steps in Robin's development." I tilted my head as if this would help me to see how. Denton continued …

"The prototype Robin was designed for use at interviewing candidates for a job. It was programmed to ask questions to a certain formula and to then evaluate the candidate's responses. Were they evasive, uncertain or even downright untruths."

"Yes," I agreed. "This was an early use of AI. I had some involvement in that."

"And you know better than I, maybe, that from there …"

"The police picked up on it as a pretty good way of interrogating suspects," I supplied.

Denton nodded cheerfully. "So, we have our own super-sleuth and a guardian, or companion if you like, familiar with its capabilities."

I nodded now that my mental clouds were clearing. "OK. So, I'm a Dr Watson, then. Will he have already been programmed with the right sort of questions - and is there already a suspect? Oh, and …" I rushed another question in before anyone could start talking, "… are we sure it's a homicide and if so, how do we know that?"

There was a longer pause now and they looked at each other. Who was going to answer, they were deciding. It was telepathically concluded that would be James Sutheridge.

The wrinkles on his face seemed to smooth out a little. His eyes narrowed slightly and he ran his tongue across his lips. No nod. No slight smile. He began ...

"I'll start by giving you a rundown of the set up on Mars at this moment. There are just two teams there and they are working from two base camps which are about five miles - eight clicks if you prefer - apart. One is out near the edge of a crater. Two guys are on that and I'll come to them in a minute. The other camp is larger and built into the lower slope of a small mountain. It has always been the main UN base on Mars and it was set up about ten years ago. Its personnel have changed, do change, frequently. As of now, we have one dead body there and two others, very much alive and very much worried, of course. They're eager for our team to arrive and sort out the mess. But that won't be for about another 75 days."

"Wow!" I interrupted. "Not 5 to 8 months then?"

"Right. I told you we have quicker space travel now. To carry on ... The dead person is an Israeli male. The other two are a German male and a US female. I'll give you a fuller run-down on all these in a bit but, to cut down on all our questions and answers, here are thumbnails of everyone there with nice pictures. Study them well now - but it still won't prepare you for when you meet them."

He passed across several A4 sheets of paper. After a cursory glance, I stowed them away in my folder - I didn't have the luxury of a brief case, especially one with UN stamped on it in gold lettering.

"I'll look at them tonight," I suggested. "Are we ending this briefing today?"

James answered in the affirmative and Rick Templar threw in, "A tea break in, say, another hour so, I suggest we push on."

I picked up my little note book by the spine and considered what I'd written but my mind was circling the whole scenario …

"If there are just two suspects at the base camp it seems that our super-sleuth should have no problem pointing his android finger at the guilty party. Yes? Plus, one small crime scene where it all took place. Sounds like a doddle for Robin." I looked at each in turn.

James shook his head. "No crime scene is ever a doddle. You'll probably be surprised how just two characters can wrap it all up in confusing facts or, more likely, invention."

"But, I thought all murders boil down to motive. Surely, the motive will quickly become apparent. How many motives could there be?" I spread my hands.

Rick Templar gave a low growl which somehow signified amusement. "The two survivors at the main base camp are man and woman. I bet that's one motive that's high in the statistics. Sex. Then, there's inter-job clashes together with inter-state. The thought, a Jew and a German put together springs to mind. Plus, responsibilities: how's the command structure working out on the base - or, isn't it?"

James added to this from his vast experience. "In the early days of space flight, exploration and all that, the rich countries like America led the way and, consequently, the whole of the mission team would have this uniting factor in their minds - we're all in the same outfit. And they were proud of it too. I'm not saying everything ran smoothly, but the niggles, the mistakes, the catastrophes, were eased away by that factor of togetherness. Now? Well, we're a mixed bag. The United Nations doesn't achieve any uniting."

I nodded at that.

James continued, "So, that is another possible motive."

The ball went back into Rick's court - "On top of clear cut motives, consider this ... Having complex tasks to perform on a completely alien world is *extremely* stressful. A flash point can arise out of nowhere with little provocation. Just think back to your own outburst this morning ..." I reddened slightly ..."and that was in a safe, warm meeting room in the heart of London."

I was surprised when Denton enlightened us still further. "Also, you may not know this, but the Israeli was *very, very* rich and he liked to flaunt around a huge diamond ring on his finger. I wouldn't take bets it's still there when you arrive."

"Well, it'll still be there on Mars," I countered. "Sandman'll soon sniff it out."

Somehow our tea needs had been communicated to others in the building and this was now the cause for a break. I didn't really want it to stop now we were in full flow but James had to take a leak anyway. He scraped his chair aside and left us. I deliberately moved next to Denton.

"I'm afraid I don't really buy your robbery motive," I said.

He turned with a grin. "Neither do I," he said. "But, you never know."

When we were all set to continue, I began wondering about another facet of the Martian set-up and it wasn't totally connected with the murder - it was as much about just satisfying my scientific curiosity.

"The other party," I began. "The two guys who are exploring the surface ... for water or minerals or whatever. I take it they won't be involved in any investigation. Too far away? Now ..."

James was shaking his head. "We don't know that for sure. They'll need alibis too."

"Tell me," I said, straying now to satisfy my plain, scientific curiosity. "Have they found anything at all to do with what early Mars was like? The Press has mentioned 'bones'. What kind of bones still hasn't been revealed." I must have shown my excitement as I leaned forward. "Any from early Martian civilisations? Any artefacts or remains of buildings?"

James nodded repeatedly but didn't smile. Not the murder maybe but this was also serious stuff. "I think the media has covered a few basics already but I can tell that you think our boys should have come up with more by now. Yes?"

I nodded, secretly urging him on.

He continued. "We all know the basics of Martian pre-history, if I can use that terminology. Mars lost most of its atmosphere millions of years ago so, today it's thin and mostly CO_2. Point-two percent oxygen is all that's left. But the evidence for a once-vibrant planet is there to see and our satellites had told us the story of vast water courses long before we actually got there." He paused to hitch up a trouser leg. "Our search teams were not sited to look for signs of fossilised flora and fauna. It was all about the water and minerals that are still there. But, even so, yes; they've found bones and other fossils ..." He paused, perhaps deliberately teasing me for it was obvious what I wanted to know. "Sorry to disappoint you, Dave, but we haven't found any signs of ancient Martian civilisations at all. Zilch. Nada."

"Oh," was all I could manage.
But now Denton took up the Martian history lesson ...

"However, we - the archaeologists - have found plenty of bones, fossilised, of course, and these are of *intelligent* life forms."

My drooping spirits were magically revived.

"Dinosaurs!" he said.

"But …" I didn't know how to progress this but James took up the story. He explained …

"Think about it. There was once an abundance of water here, a good atmosphere, seasonal warmth - the ideal for plant growth and this, of course, is food for whatever creatures succeed. The dinosaurs on Earth had the same resources and became hugely successful. If there hadn't been that horrendous meteor catastrophe - horrendous for them, but not for us and our mammalian companions - they would still be ruling Earth."

"And on Mars …?" I egged on.

"No meteor but another, slower, destroyer of life."

"So, what you're saying is … the last dominant species of life on Mars was dinosaurs. Wow! What a thought."

Rick had to join in. "The dinosaurs on Mars would not have been nearly as gigantic as on Earth, though. The reason for that was that our early plant life grew in a sort of greenhouse. It was gigantic, flourishing like we can't imagine. And, the more food, the more growth for the eaters of that food." He smiled. "My kids always wanted to be big so, I used to tell them, 'Eat a big breakfast and you'll grow big.' It worked too."

James nodded. "I had a grandad who owned an old country cottage. It was made for folk who struggled to eat well each year. The number of times I banged my head on the low doorframes. It seemed like it was made for midgets."

We could have been drawing to an end with this revelation about the Martian past but a bigger piece of info was still to be dropped into my lap.

"Ever wondered if we would ever get away from the necessity for space suits when we walked outside on Mars?" asked Rick in his slow growl.

I thought about this. "Sure. But I read something about producing oxygen. Don't know the details but I guess they'll find a way. Mars with blue skies, eh?"

Rick looked enigmatic. "There's another way and we're trying it right now. Want the details?"

"Of course," I encouraged but I couldn't think of this other way.

"It all started when we got so far down with our under-sea explorations on Earth that we were into water at such depths that it contained no oxygen. None at all."

"Pretty lifeless, then," I chipped in.

"Actually, and amazingly, no. Creatures were found living down there - and this will stagger you - that are multi-cellular. Not simple, bacteria-type but much more complex. Maybe not fish but, - this is the point - they actually have an entirely different metabolism which produces electric energy without breaking down oxygen. Can you see where this is going?"

"No," I said bluntly.

"I'm not surprised. Where it went is that, by messing with DNA and by using complex surgical techniques that weren't dreamed of fifty years ago, our science has produced ..."

"A bloody monster!" I couldn't help interjecting.

Denton corrected me. "No; a Martian."

It should have been the grand finale but, not quite. I felt a little sick as the mind-pictures from old sci-fi horror films crowded in. I couldn't resist a last expression of disgust …

"And, I suppose you - the UN progressive science department or whatever they're called - have this hideous creature in some kind of Martian mock-up, testing out its capabilities." I packed my little note-book away.

"You're nearly right about that, David," said James, rather tiredly. "But your monster - our man-made Martian - is one of the two guys at camp 2. He's probably out right now, feeling quite at home, looking for whatever is just under the surface of Mars."

That ended the session and, finally, left me speechless.

··········

✧ ✧ ✧

As I plodded down the worn steps leading from the UN building onto the street, my mind was so busy churning over all that had been said that I almost bumped into James Sutheridge. He had paused to flag down a taxi but did not go ahead with that when he saw I was there.

"Dave!" he said. "I was just thinking about you. I don't think you got all the answers in there, did you?"

I lifted my folder ruefully. All it contained was my little notebook and the A4 descriptive profile pages.

"Not really, James. We never did get around to talking about the main event, the murder. Not to mention the additional person, or is it more than one, who is to make the journey to Mars with me."

It was still struggling to rain and the few drops which spattered down onto his suit seemed to bring him to a decision. He shook his shoulders and said, "Look. What say we have a drink together before you get your train home - Nottingham isn't it? I reckon we could just about clear up the final items."

"Sounds a plan to me."

The taxi, which he insisted on paying for, took us away from the area of large, official-looking buildings to a more lived-in district. I didn't know London so, just where we were I had no idea. I didn't ask.

The tavern we finally arrived at was deceptive - its rather worn appearance disguised a slick efficiency that I quite admired.

"Wine or beer?" he queried and we finished up with a bottle of Merlot between us, very smooth and, I suspected, costing a lot more than I would have paid. Knowing something of James's past, that of a celebrated astronaut, I reckoned he could not only afford it but had also refrained from taking me to his club to avoid embarrassing me. I'd never had enough 'champers' to gain a taste for it, anyway.

When we were comfortably settled in a cosy corner and had taken a sip or two, I decided to take the lead ...

"Tell me about the so-called murder, James, if you will. Was it a bloody affair? A stabbing or ..." I deliberately tailed off for he would soon paint the picture, I knew.

He gave a supressed laugh. "If you have a mental picture of some gory murder scene, then, David my friend, you are in more ways than one, a million miles from the truth. No blood. No injury to the body." He sipped his wine. "Quite simply, our rich Israeli was suffocated in the airlock."

I gasped. "Then how did it get classified as a murder? It sounds to me like an accident."

"Ah!" James twisted the side of his mouth. "Are you familiar with the Hoyles airlock?"

I shook my head. "I've never used any type of airlock. They *are* used at Intel Robotics but only to protect some of the more delicate components. Or in the test labs. By the time I get to handle component parts, they are fully sealed and ready to go."

"The airlocks we use on Mars are a different cup-of-tea. Basically the same idea as most airlocks but they have built- in security which not only stops both doors, the entrance and the exit, being opened simultaneously - most do that anyway as a general principle - but they are monitored by video and by sound alerts. If a door is open for more than 20 seconds, all hell lets loose."

"So, what went wrong?"

"The outer door stayed open but no alarm sounded. And when Helen, the base commander, realised Ezra Pensak - that's the Israeli - should be inside the module ..." James stopped and gave an elaborate shrug. Then he continued, because I was looking quite blank. "Outer door open, well over the time limit yet no alarm whatsoever. When he'd been brought in, she thought, like you, a malfunction of the circuitry controlling the doors. Also, no alarms."

"Can you explain in a little more detail how the airlock works?"

"Sorry, old son," and he shook his head. "You'll have to ask Helen when you get there - or read all the manuals before you go."

"Mmh. I'll try to read up on known failures. But, who cried 'wolf'? Who ...?"

"That was Helen. With all the built-in safety features these airlocks have, she couldn't believe it was an accident, a malfunction."

"Did the German go along with that?"

"I should think 'not'. Well, if you look at the situation - if she is saying it was death by murder, she's almost saying he did it. And the converse puts her as the murderer."

"But, this is a crazy situation. Only two likely suspects and - surely she never contacted UN Mission Control and said in so many words 'A man has died here and I believe he was murdered'."

"Of course not." James poured another drink for each of us before continuing. "She reported it as an accident but, the UN has a code system like many police forces do. She just finished her report by saying, 'I believe this to be a code HX' - H for homicide and X for unknown. Hans, the German, wouldn't know this."

"But ... I'm assuming he read it ... it would be natural for him to ask her, 'Heh, what's this code HX about?' I take it he's no fool."

"And neither is she, I can assure you. She'd have had time to come up with something. The airlock is a Hoyles - how about H for Hoyles and X for, say, external door? She had time to come up with something more believable."

I didn't know whether it was the wine but I grinned at him. "Your first effort is believable enough for me."

He raised his half-full glass in a silent toast.

He left me for a loo trip and I used the time to think about my next query - who else might be making the trip. Would he know?

He came back in a few minutes muttering, "That's easier."

I reminded him of the next question by making a suggestion. "I met a rather, er, attractive UN lady when I had my first briefing. I don't suppose you know if she could be the one assigned for the final place on the Mars ship?"

"I think I've met her. Anna would that be? Yes, I can see why you are hoping for her company but I'm afraid it's another disappointment for David Harper. It is a female who is going, though. One I've not met. Oh, and her name isn't Susan either: it's Rita McKinley. I'm afraid I cannot tell you much about her other than she is a long-time United Nations executive officer. Don't groan, David; drink up your wine. She was a professional wrestler - no, I'm just joking there but, she was some sort of Olympic athlete. I can't remember whether runner or swimmer, though, if she's going to Mars, I would think not the latter. I haven't an A4 on her I'm afraid.

I seemed to remember matching his consumption of the Merlot but I couldn't seem to figure out clearly why he was acting intelligently and normally whereas I seemed to have difficulty in, well, just figuring things out.

I somehow managed a vague idea of my little notebook questions so I ventured ....

"And what is to be her purpose in going?"

He puzzled over that one for a short time, then, "I really don't know, old sport. She is quite talented, though. A cool cookie, as the Americans might say. My guess is that she'll take charge of the whole shebang. But that doesn't tell us what she'll do."

I nodded.

"You were wondering about the flight details," he asked. He couldn't have been spying into my little book, I reasoned.

He had worked out that I wasn't alert enough to continue so, he carried on, no doubt hoping I would remember some of what he said, at least.

"You'll blast off - not quite the right expression, I know - from New Mexico. The commercial spaceport there has been extended and modified to suit true space missions. Not to mention it was bought out by the UN. You will arrive there by a special UN flight from Heathrow the day after tomorrow. Get injections and clothing at the space-port. Maintenance equipment for your work - if required - will have been loaded into the space vehicle. As Denton said, 'you won't have anything to worry about.'

"Well, that may be so but, what'll I do on the flight? What is standard for non-participating passengers?"

"That's a nice piece of terminology, David. I'll have to remember that."

"So - what will I do for the whole trip? 75 days is a long time. Do I read? Look at videos? Read the manuals? Cut my toe nails?"

"No, David. You do what you are so nearly practising now. You sleep. It may be too early to say it now but, pleasant dreams."

··········

✧ ✧ ✧ ✧

The lady who had just walked across to join me on the lift-off pad at the UN's space centre in New Mexico smiled and held out a slim, tanned hand.

"Rita McKinley," she introduced herself. "And you must be David Harper. Do you prefer David or Dave? I guess you don't want Mr Harper." Her smile widened into a grin. "Seems like we'll be travelling companions on this long journey to Mars."

"Uh,uh. I usually get the simplified form, Dave - maybe because I'm a simple sort of guy, but I answer to either one."

She nodded and turned to look at the monstrous contraption in front of us which I had been studying.

"Wha'dya think of it," she asked, with deliberate slang, nodding at the monster.

I rubbed my stubbly chin. "Well, if some cranky sculptor had been asked to weld together two large bedsteads, a ship's cargo container and a beer fermentation cooker with about five hundred pieces of aluminium tubing - I think he'd have finished up with something similar."

"Yes," she agreed. "It doesn't look to me capable of getting past the moon let alone the next 40-odd million miles but tomorrow we'll find out."

"Nice to hear that said not in kilometres," I said. "I like to think of distances - long distances, that is - in miles."

"And that helps you visualise what 40 or 50 million is?" she smiled, with a gentle, teasing sarcasm.

Now she visually searched the small number of ground crew or maintenance people who were attending to the monster.

"Where's Rick, our pilot?" she asked. "I thought he was over here too."

"Oh, Rick's poking about inside," I answered. "Don't ask, doing what. There doesn't seem to be any flight control surfaces to test. I didn't know any of us were allowed into the space vehicle but it must be a new count-down system."

"He's probably checking his personal food or entertainment is properly packed," she suggested.

"I thought we all had to sleep through the journey."

"Not Rick. We can't have a pilot sleeping on the job," she chided with more amusement.

I was thinking, she seems pretty relaxed. I wasn't. I was plain scared. She helped to ease it a little, though.

"I don't understand this 'sleeping' thing," I said. "How can we sleep for, what, almost 3 months? Seems to me it will be more like an induced coma."

"No; it is sleep. We take special pills that will effect periodic sleep patterns. There will be a pattern to it but you'll need to ask Rick about that."

"Sounds like a women's thing," I joked.

"Mission crew don't use them but there aren't any on our trip unless you count Rick. Their trips have plenty of experiments to keep them occupied - usually how plants or tissue behave in zero gravity. That sort of thing. The consumption of food and oxygen is therefore justified. We don't do anything useful until we get there."

I thought this over. "I'm still not convinced I'll do anything useful on Mars," I said. "They said that I'm sort of robot-sitting. What can that mean?"

To my surprise she was able to give me, at last, a more meaningful explanation ...

"It was agreed many years ago - and I'm a little surprised you aren't au fait with this - or maybe you are - that androids or robots with artificial intelligence capability must be, what's the word? - 'attended' by a human. This is because their intelligence …"

The mid-morning sun was beginning to make its power felt - on me at any rate. Rita seemed impervious. I had to make a suggestion …

"Shall we go across to the café building? I could murder a cold drink. I'll be glad to hear the rest of your explanation then."

She nodded agreement and we strolled the short distance to shade and refreshment, taking in the smart yet functional modern buildings. Further away were the space port buildings which served the paying customers who were just into orbital flights. Between us and those buildings were the super-long runways, necessary for the re-usable space craft which they would fly in to land comfortably.

Armed with iced drinks, we sat down and I was braced eagerly for her telling me what she knew about the reason for me being here. First, she gave a rueful smile.

"I don't know how long ago it was that no-smoking rules were drafted, but - a cigarette would have gone nicely with this," and she lifted and waved her drink.

"Just a minute," I said, inclining my head to one side. "I heard you were an Olympic athlete; a runner. Surely smoking wasn't part of your daily training routine."

"That was then and this is now," she smiled. "Anyway, I only got a bronze. Maybe a weed back then would have pushed me over the line a bit quicker."

"Well," I matched her grin. "It depends which weed you're talking about. Back then plenty of them did take the weed that pushed them over."

She nodded a little sadly at this and sipped her drink. That would have to do this time, I thought. After a short pause, perhaps reflecting on her past, she continued with why I was there.

"'Attended' by a human, I think I was saying." I nodded. "And me being surprised you didn't know this - that because artificial intelligence doesn't extend to human-like perception or feelings and so on - that simply programming an AI robot may leave it with, er, deficiencies in its thinking. For example: if I may presume to use our own Martian incident as a case in point ..."

I nodded for her to continue.

"Robin, our AI detective, having been given all the facts about the death of Ezra in the airlock - and, having interviewed Helen and Hans and become aware, through tonal responses, of, say, hatred directed from Hans to Ezra." I nodded for her to continue, " ... and, say, Robin also knows that Hans carried out some maintenance adjustments to the interlocking doors of the airlock - With his built-in programming for making a sound conclusion from all this data, he will recommend that Hans be arrested on a code S1."

I was absolutely staggered.

"Is this ...?" I began.

"No, Dave. It's a purely hypothetical possibility."

"I've come across this UN code thing before," I said. "What on Earth is a code S1? Or, shouldn't I know?"

"A code S1 is Suspect number one," she said.

"OK; but now - why a human attendant?"

She leaned back and smiled. "Because Robin isn't capable, or at least not so easily capable, of discerning a factor that you would have become aware of."

I waited.

"That Hans is a homosexual. That, in fact, he has strong feelings of love, not hatred, for Ezra. Robin has correctly detected strong passionate feelings from Hans to Ezra but, his programming has not accurately interpreted the true situation. Also, because this is a frustrated feeling and because he wants to hide it from Helen, Ezra frequently makes disparaging remarks about a man he certainly doesn't hate. Robin misreads the intent of these remarks."

"And, all this is absolutely fiction?" I confirmed.

Rita nodded and smiled. "Absolutely - as far as I know," she affirmed. "So, you see how a human being present would see the true situation."

"Sounds like it should have been a code S5," I joked. We both grinned and finished our drinks.

"I'm glad I've found out at last why I'm here," I said, and I breathed out heavily.

....

✫ ✫ ✫ ✫ ✫

Last day. Last breakfast. Last hours of familiarity with a world I knew. Would it be 'last' with that meaning of total finality? My mind dwelt on this with a nerve-jangling insistence.

Rick and Rita approached and my opened palm invited them to join me.

"I'll bet your nervous intensity reading is near the critical," grinned Rick.

I somehow choked out a mumbled, "You bet." I wondered at his apparent calm and continued, "I've always been amazed at the way you pro astronauts seem so relaxed and jokey just before you climb into a spacecraft. How d'you manage it? Do you take pills or something?"

Rita was sorting out her meal on the tray she had brought to the table. She nodded. "Tell us the secret, Rick," she said. "Tell us so that Dave and I can maybe relax just a mite."

Rick nodded more seriously. "When a would-be astronaut begins his training, the careless grin is just a front: he's as scared as anyone else. However, in that training he has to face plenty of scary situations but, he overcomes them one by one until, heh, guess what - scary situations; life-threatening moments, are just a part of his everyday life. So then, miraculously, what's to fear? If something goes wrong, you sort it - or you don't live long enough to wonder why you couldn't sort it. Surprisingly perhaps, those grinning, joking faces you see on videos are genuine. Those guys are now enjoying this sort of life. They're getting the chance to do things you only dream of doing when you're a kid."

Rita swallowed some food before pointing out dryly, "But we've not had that training."

There was really no comeback to that so, Rick got on with his meal.

After the food had disappeared and before preparing ourselves for the final stages of countdown, we did try to relax. We sat in surprisingly comfortable wicker chairs. Rick had a newspaper but I didn't let him read much before beginning more questions.

"Rick; I'm still puzzled and wondering about a few other things."

He laid the paper aside. "Go ahead then, Dave. What else is troublin' you?"

"Radiation. There's a lot of people who seem convinced that we can't cope with all the radiation we'll get out in space - and on the red planet. How is that being dealt with – I presume it is?"

The pilot didn't look at all worried, I thought, anxiously awaiting his reply. His explanation soon showed why. I'd been worrying perhaps a little too much.

"Forget radiation on Mars. That's the most easily dealt with. The rovers have shown it isn't as bad as was figured initially. I don't want to get too technical but, we're talking fractions of millisieverts here."

I looked blank and Rita chipped in with, "That's how radiation is measured."

"To tackle it over a longish period," Rick carried on "and now I'm talking about Marsbase One: If we placed enough soil on top of the base it would shield anyone inside as effectively as if they were on Earth. But we don't need a soil-shifting exercise because what we've found in abundance on Mars are caverns and fissures into the mountains. The amount of natural cover from those is plenty thick enough to give all the protection that's needed."

"Mmmh," I responded. "But what about in space - the journey bit?"

Rick nodded. "With the new method of propulsion we now have, weight won't be a problem. So, it's just a matter of piling enough shielding around the ship. That covers most things in more ways than one."

"But, not entirely?" Rita slipped in.

"No, not entirely. Solar flares are the remaining worry."

"So?" she pursued.

"We now have a space weather centre and it's pretty good at forecasting unusual solar activity." Rick twisted his lips. "Notice that I said 'unusual'. At the moment, if we get advanced warning we just don't make a trip." He spread his tanned and freckled arms wide. "And this trip has got the all clear."

"Thank goodness for that," I muttered.

"Anything else?" Rick queried, looking at me but then swinging his gaze to Rita. I thought she seemed to know most of the answers so was surprised when she spoke.

"What about these violent dust storms they have on Mars, Rick?" she asked. Her brows creased up. "Don't they sometimes extend over the whole planet?"

He nodded but developed a gentle smile. "They sometimes do," he said in his soft growl. "But forget the 'violent' part - you've been watching too much sci-fi. Most of these storms are not planet coverers and the worst of them are only about 60 miles per hour - about half the strength of one of our gales on Earth. And there's another factor. Because of the thin atmosphere on Mars they don't build up the kinetic energy that our storms do. No, sandstorms in themselves are a no-worry."

"But?" This came from me. There was obviously a kicker.

Rick started what was to be his final lesson on Martian topography that day. "It isn't the sand *storms*," he began. "It's the sand itself - and the blowing about doesn't help at whatever speed. You see, Martian sand is very fine - and it sticks. First job every day is cleaning the solar panels. Then, through the day and when we pack up, it's cleaning out, vacuuming any movable bits that the sand will be clogging up if left. It's a bugger of a nuisance, to be blunt."

We soon broke up after this and went our separate ways to do whatever people do before a space mission. For some, that might be making their peace with a god. For me, it was having a damn good bath, for it would only be the sponge baths system once we were up and away. There was little more to learn. We had been given the exact details and routine. We were as ready, mentally and physically, as we would ever be. At eleven-thirty we would be suited-up for the trip and given the equivalent of a pre-op relaxing pill. The outfits we would all wear, including Robin but not, of course, Sandman, would be one-piece, zip from neck to crotch, material that was soft and flexible but hard-wearing. Colour, white. UN insignia in gold on top pocket. We would take off wearing space helmets which were fitted with intercoms but these would be removed soon into the flight upon a signal from Rick. We would all be seated horizontally on reclinable, padded seats in 2 rows of 2. That included Robin but, since Sandman would be strapped to the floor of the cabin, there would be a spare seat for Rick if he wanted to leave his place in a forward control recess to join us. In his pilot's recess he would be faced by rows of dials, lights and switches and have control of the lander rockets. For 60 minutes we would be entirely in his hands and that of ground control.

I had now learned also about the sleep routine - at commencement and end of flight we would have what might be called a 'normal' week. The first one would give us the opportunity to learn standard procedures for eating and for personal hygiene. After week one, we would have our induced sleep for 5 days, then awaken for 2, and so on. I had been surprised to find out that there are some people on Earth who already sleep, to a certain degree 'normally', for 5 days. But I also learned just how complex sleep is with its different levels of brain activity. I'd been curious but had decided it was too complex a subject to waste time on. Good Lord, even the experts seemed to have trouble grasping all the consequences.

I didn't know much about countdown procedures at that time. Later I was to learn just how much the total countdown time had been reduced by us having no liquid propellant. From when we were strapped in, there would be just 60 minutes before lift-off. We would be on 'T60 and holding.' Satisfactorily bedded down and locked in, it would go to T60 and counting. Then counts to T40, T20 and T10, when there would be another and final hold. Internal systems would be ON with just a minute and a half remaining and lift off or simply 'GO' would follow, being the usual Mars missions' signal to leave behind good, old Earth.

If all went well, upon Rick's signal at approximately 10 minutes after GO, we would report to him how fine we all felt, remove our helmets and adjust our seats into upright

- and breathe in deeply and thankfully. Red planet - and murderer - here we come!

....

✧ ✧ ✧ ✧ ✧

The lift off - it certainly couldn't have been described as a 'blast off' - had gone well. I was now getting to feel almost normal. Rick, Rita and I chatted in a desultory way about everything imaginable, most of it, surprisingly perhaps, not about Mars or what would happen when we got there. Maybe we'd had our fill of that in the preliminary briefings. So, we talked about friends and family and what might have taken place in their lives in the 7 or 8 months that we would be gone from them. Also, what might take place in world politics or the vast arena of sport.

I brooded over Nottingham Forest football team's chances as they would be into a new season. I thought about Sue, of course, and whether she would then have a new boyfriend. Would Colin still be at Intel-Robotics?

I also thought about how my health and my body would cope with the possibilities of micro-organism infections on board the spaceship - and on a new world too. I wasn't enamoured by the toilet and sponge bath hygiene systems but the food was pretty well worked out these days with trays of meals in heatable, disposable bags, the items contained therein being more frequently solid rather than liquidised and reasonably tasty. The spoon was the main eating utensil but I had always been a spoon-man rather than, say, chopsticks.

Of course, we all marvelled at the black sky with its ultra-bright stars and, for some time, with the receding bulk of our blue Earth despite having seen videos of it for many years. After all, this was for real.

The windows were, a central one forward giving the pilot a view ahead; and elongated ones on each side at head height. As we sped away from Earth I had thought we should have had a rear-facing one but it was the left-side window which was filled by Earth's bulk. Presumably this was because we weren't travelling in a straight line. The whole trip, I reminded myself, was about orbits and curved trajectories.

The other thing which I noticed didn't quite match the videos of astronauts in space was that objects did not float freely. Because we were still accelerating, and would be for about half the trip, there was a force, albeit not very strong, pulling everything towards, mainly, the rear end of our cabin. Later this direction would change and cause a strange disorientating effect.

As the time for our first long period of sleep neared I turned to Rita who sat on my right and I grinned.

"This long sleep pattern that's coming up," I said. It reminds me of a thought that hit me once, about a couple of years ago. Most people perhaps don't ever think about it but, as you'll find out maybe, I think of all sorts of weird things." I paused, still smiling broadly and she waited patiently. "The maths is easy enough once you get the thought into your head but, have you ever thought about how long we sleep in our lives?" She just blinked at me, perhaps starting the maths. "Well," I carried on, "Take someone not excessively old, say 60 - they could easily have slept for 20 years! If you took it a step further and said to an old man of 90, 'What did you do for most of your life?' and he came back with, 'Just slept for 30 years of it.' Well, don't you think that's incredible? "

She laughed. "You're right; I'd never thought about it. Even our little chunks of 5 days seem not quite right."

We were soon to begin this system of making the time pass. Also, of course, to conserve our limited energy supply. As I drifted away at the beginning of the initial 7-day cycle, the accompanying rather soothing effect supplied by the ship was a faint rumbling sound that was all pervasive and an accompanying slight vibration. I still found myself hazily thinking, 'Whatever am I here for?' as I went into my first deep sleep.

··········

We were getting close now; close to the big, red disc that filled the black sky. All three of us had been thunderstruck when it first crept into view and we couldn't stop getting out of our seats and standing, totally awed, for yet another look. It may have still looked like videos we'd seen taken from orbiters but, somehow, the knowledge that this was the real thing sent electrical impulses down one's spine.

"Get a load o' that," gasped the usually nonchalant Rick. "Look at that damned huge valley."

"And it will get bigger," Rita said.

I still found time to worry.

"Are all the lights green?" I asked Rick. "You haven't got time for sight-seeing yet."

Our pilot blew out some air forcefully. "I'm not missing this, kiddo. Don't worry, this baby could land itself."

I countered with a snort of my own. "Yeah, and this baby could blow itself up with rather a big bang. Haven't you heard the expression, 'exploded upon impact'?"

He looked across at me to see if I looked worried but he still grinned.

Rita still smiled too but I thought it just a wee bit forced.

Rick decided to settle our worries. "Remember an old song that is sometimes still played … 'Ground control to Major Tom..'? The good news, folks, is that we are even now under the unerring guidance of Ground Control. Ground Control doesn't mean Helen Anderson the base commander either. It's a pretty sophisticated computer that'll control our touch-down. Never heard of artificial intelligence, Dave?" he finished with a dig at me.

But, of course, I had to find a comeback … "And from what I do know about it, I'd sooner it be Helen that has taken control."

Rita couldn't resist a snigger.

Never-the-less, Rick dutifully re-sat on his special seat and even strapped himself in and began to fasten on his helmet. "You'll all be pleased to know that, yes, all lights are green, er," he suddenly sounded worried … "except for this red one." But as we paused with our own helmets dangling we could see his expression.

"You blighter," burst out Rita.

Perhaps we needed a bit of humour at just this moment because both Rita and I now realised we were no longer orbiting; we were going straight down, though the speed was easing off. We strapped ourselves back onto our seats and made them horizontal. Helmets were clipped back on. We managed to twist our heads, though, to watch the outer view camera.

Mountains and craters and gullies grew larger at an astonishing rate. Then another reality came as the uneven surface changed to show all the rocks and boulders which were strewn about. Dust began to swirl beneath us as our only rockets, the small landers, ignited and began to set our 375-ton bulk down as gently as could be.

Then, a moment which was somehow sheer magic: total stillness.

....

✧ ✧ ✧ ✧ ✧ ✧ ✧

I couldn't have been more excited, I thought, than if I'd been one of the first men to make a footprint on the moon. Looking at both Rita and Rick, each had an intensity about them which even the slight distortion from their helmets and the bulk of their space suits failed to hide. We were still going to be three of the very first privileged few to have taken that colossal 40-million-mile ride to another planet. And, I thought, not just any planet - Mars had a mystique which had gripped mankind since he had first looked to the heavens and realised that one of our nearest neighbours was red. Then, for a long period of years, his imagination had run wild with the thought of living neighbours on that red world. Both fantasy and cold reason had grappled with what kind of living neighbours we might have, the cold reason thwarted by the extremely slow accumulation of knowledge. All right, we could now smile at the thought of the canals on Mars once propounded, yet, I realised, despite the fact that we'd had machines and humans trundling across the Martian surface for several years now, the possibility of some form of life here had still not been totally ruled out. Amazing!

Thus, we three hustled towards the ship's airlock to test it for the first time and then to leave our footprints in the newly disturbed red sand around the ship. I realised I was trembling but it wasn't fear. We would then have the second airlock - the killer airlock, I thought, into Marsbase One - to traverse. Of course, I had no qualms about it; it had been well and truly tested on a daily basis before we even began our journey here. Several new people to meet then and, soon to follow, the tricky business of examining evidence and interrogating suspects or witnesses. I frowned at the thought of that.

....

Our long-suffering - that is the way I thought of it - spaceship had landed on a flat area maybe 3 or 4 hundred yards from our new home, Marsbase One. Well done, Rick.

Everything about us we scrutinised and assessed, then we strode off towards our new home. Walking in this low gravity was weird but, somehow, everything was weird. We didn't mind - we were there! We would have to mind the few rocks laying about but we set out at a fair rate towards the base's airlock doors, reached by a shallow downward incline into the mountain wherein nestled the base. Although not long after the Martian midday and with the small sun still high, my first impression was of how dull it seemed. I knew from our briefings on Earth that this was caused by the seasonal effect. At another time of the Martian year it could have been quite bright.

Somewhat belatedly it seemed, a metallic voice sounded in our helmets …

"Welcome, all. Welcome to Mars."

Rick replied for all of us, "Glad to be here, Helen. Put the kettle on."

We other two smiled at that. Typical Rick.

At the gleaming aluminium doors of the airlock, which were taller than I had anticipated - of course, I reasoned, furniture and large structural parts had needed to be carried in when it was first built - we paused and Rick pressed a button under some sort of sealing material. Not rubber, I guessed. While we waited, like children who'd been carol singing, for the door to open, we looked around and I noted that it was quite a small drift of sand at the bottom of the door. Thinking of how it must blow about, it seemed, as we had been told, that it would have been cleaned away recently. Then we were in. A very brightly lit room. There were several closed lockers all around with symbols on the doors to show what they contained - spare space suits, digging tools, various vacuum cleaning devices, etc. There were benches too and we sat down and began to disrobe as we had previously practised on Earth. No-one wore personal under-garments. Everything was pre-prescribed. Because of the nature of our visit here, I was curious to examine more features of the airlock but that didn't seem quite the thing to do at this time. At last we had all donned our new and sporty-looking outfits which were long-legged trousers and loose-fitting but warm tops; no socks - which I didn't like - and trainers. For some reason or other we had our names in large letters on our backs and I felt like a pro footballer. The exit door had closed, smoothly enough, inside its 20 seconds and we were good to go. Then the door into the main section of the base opened and we faced a smiling Helen Anderson and Hans Schroeder.

    We all trouped into the main living section where hot and cold drinks and a good assortment of food was laid out on a long central table. Soon we were all feeding ourselves and chatting with excited abandon. Gosh, this feels better, I thought - quite civilised. I had half expected the other two to be here but this wasn't really a welcome party, I knew. Tan

Lee and the man-made Martian, who had apparently been quite happy to accept his given name of Alan Marsman - A Mars man, of course - were both making good use of the sunlight and favourable weather.

As the conversations dwindled and the novelty of our new home for some months to come became absorbed into reality, a rather awkward expectancy crept upon us. Helen had not been given the role of base commander for nothing, however: she quickly met the situation head on.

"Everyone!" she announced with some authority. We quietened down to hear what she would say. "I shall set out where we go from here on. If you all would kindly wait until I've finished, then we can discuss, complain, question and, even, argue. Whatever."

Silence followed but Rita nodded so she continued. "First, the command structure. I am still the Base Commander. My duties will remain as laid down in my contract, that is, to supervise any personnel using the base facilities and to maintain these facilities in good order and to settle any matters of dispute about how we operate here. So far, this system has worked very well since I've been here but I realise that new and terrible circumstances may force us to make some adjustments. However, these adjustments should not - and I will not let them - interfere with the day-to-day running of the base." She now paused and sipped a cold drink she had poured. We all sat quite still and waited for more. She soon delivered.

"Technically, Rita here; Rita McKinley, is ranked higher in the United Nations command structure than I. But here we have a situation that is forced upon us. So - there should be no conflict between us in that our jobs here are, at least they should be, meant to cover different areas of expertise. Where our different areas overlap or conflict, I shall give my fullest support and co-operation to Rita. Her task here has the top priority. She will not only command the investigation into the death of Ezra Pensak, she will make an assessment of who or what was responsible and she alone will deicide upon the outcome. I will tell you all, that she is faced with a unique responsibility and task, for the UN is still struggling ..." she glanced across at Rita to confirm this and Rita nodded, "... to apply international law to an area where that law is still being formulated. In fact, this incident may form case law for future similar tragedies." Again a sip of refreshment. "If you are bursting with questions you could shoot now but, if I may suggest - that Rita puts us all in the picture with regard to her investigation and then you've all got a complete picture to shoot it."

"Sounds a plan to me," Rick agreed instantly.

"Me too," said Hans, slowly. He had been fingering his short beard.

"What about you, Dave?" Rita asked.

I wasn't worried about being last. I liked to mull things over but I covered it by saying, "Agreed, but - a short convenience break perhaps and more drinks?"

We all got ourselves settled in a surprisingly short time. Now it was Rita's turn. She looked slowly and deliberately at each of us in turn.

"I envy Helen," she began with just a hint of a smile. "She, hopefully, will be able to carry on, almost normally. On the other hand, I'm into new territory. Fortunately I've had rather a long while to work out the system I would like to follow. One thing, my priority in fact, is to get this thing resolved as soon as possible. Although you may all agree on that, you may be surprised that my investigation starts today:

tonight actually. Just because my team will have to remain here for months until the next configuration of Earth, Mars and Sun, doesn't mean idling away any time we have."

During her first pause, Rick chipped in. "I'm glad I'll be out of it - I need a bit of 'recovery' time."

Rita shook her head. "Recover then, Rick, tonight. But tomorrow and after, Helen and I'll find you plenty to do."

Despite the serious side to it all, we all smiled. Rita continued ...

"Yes, tonight I'll start with the first questioning session - and that will be you, Helen."

I suppose this was logical but, after the 'two gals together' of a short time ago, it seemed to be almost an assault on the strongest likely point of resistance. Her cool stare at Helen also seemed rather challenging. I saw how clever it may have been for only, what? 30 minutes ago, Helen had pledged her co-operation. Top priority, she'd said. But Helen was not a top administrator for nothing - she nodded and looked quite cool.

"No problem," she said. "Actually, evening is a good time for me."

"The procedure for each of these questioning sessions ..." I noted that she was settling for that title. Mine might have been 'interrogations' but then, that's me ".... will be that our android with AI capability who we call Robin will ask most of the questions. He or It has been built and programmed with this single function in mind. And, everyone, please take note: Robin doesn't simply ask questions. He can evaluate a response not only by how it answers his question but what the subject's tonal responses give away. Police are trained to spot when someone is lying: Robin does it better."

For the first time, Hans got himself involved. "I always believed that robots, even those with artificial intelligence capabilities, cannot assess many, er, subtleties of human nature in the same way that another human can. We have an instinctive grasp of things. So, how good is this Robin going to be? I don't see it."

Rita would have been prepared for this one. "You are quite correct, Hans, in that there is a deficiency. That is why the UN legislated some years ago that a robot conducting an interrogation ..." ah, my terminology is there, after all. I felt smug, "...must be accompanied by a human. Satisfied?"

Hans nodded his acceptance.

"And, of course, I will be there in that capacity."

"Hu, hu," I coughed. "And me," I reminded her. It was time for me to be mentioned and my role in the, er, questioning sessions.

Rita looked across at me as though she had only just noticed I was there. "No, David," she said. "There is no requirement or need for two humans to be there with Robin. I fulfil the UN requirement. It'll be just me."

I was rocked back on my heels. I had been forced to separate from my girl, my job, travel millions of miles - it had been clearly spelt out why I was being forced to come here. To have a chunk of my life taken away. Now ...?
However, Helen had accepted the investigation plan. But Helen wasn't me ...

"I came because I was forced by the UN into doing a certain specialised job," I said as forcibly as I could. "So, in line with my appointment, I shall attend each questioning session." ...I was prepared to let her have her title, " ... I shall ..."

She cut me off. "You may be very knowledgeable about AI, David, but you have not been trained in interrogation techniques, so …"

"So - I shall still be there. What I was trained for will still be applicable."

"And what if I insist - order you, if you wish, - that you do not …"

"And, what if I insist that I'll be there. Question is - how will you prevent me?"

It was an impasse. Maybe she had figured that, with everyone else being there, her authority would, somehow, be upheld. She had miscalculated however. She hadn't factored in my stubbornness. I watched the muscles in her jaw tighten.

How would she play it? I didn't underestimate her but I knew she was out on a limb. There were no UN police here to act as enforcers. Eventually she gave an almost imperceptible nod.

"OK. You have my permission to attend. But you will not interfere with the questioning process."

The 'my permission' bit was to salvage her authority. I'd won and we both knew it. My only worry was, would she harbour vindictive plans for me. My only disappointment was, what needed to be and could have been a happy relationship was now destroyed. Just to close my thinking on all this, I dug up a typical man's closing thought - any sexual possibilities had been reduced by 50 percent. It would be a long bleak period until I could return home.

....

✩ ✩ ✩ ✩ ✩ ✩ ✩ ✩

Mars time 6.30 pm., day 1. Place; Helen's personal quarters. Present: Helen, seated on her bed and looking totally relaxed and, I have to say, quite attractive; Rita, Robin and me facing her. Robin stood very (intimidatingly?) close in front of Helen, Rita and I, both perhaps trying to relax after our confrontation, sat on flimsy-looking collapsible chairs. I looked around the room noting family photos, a couple of diplomas and a few knick-knacks. She wasn't into artificial flowers and we - the early explorers and base-builders, that is - had not managed to grow the real thing yet. Food plants were the priority.

"Ok; shall we begin?" said Rita. It was rather rhetorical so she immediately pressed a small controller in the palm of her hand. Robin began to earn his keep, ha, ha.

"For the record, my name is Robin," he began in the short, clipped tone he had used to call me a liar some months ago. His strange eyes stared unblinkingly at Helen. "I am a United Nations interrogation device ..." This was a new one on me, "... number ..." there followed a quick burst of sound which I knew was 'variable/superfast', the secret transmission system which made his designation unreadable, "...and my function on this mission is to assist in the examination of three humans and another living creature to ascertain the circumstances pertaining to the decease of Ezra Pensak here at Marsbase One. For the record, the date and time of this first interview is fourteen-dash-ten-dash-twenty-thirty-eight and my first interviewee is Base Commander, Helen Anderson …"

I waited with bated breath.

Robin continued. "For the record, would you please confirm that you are Helen Anderson and give your date of birth. Then, would you please state you UN job title and give a short description of your work function here on Marsbase One."

Helen took up her part in the proceedings by answering quite smoothly. At the same time, I noticed with some admiration, she stared back into the dead eyes of her interrogator with icy concentration.

"Yes, I am Helen Anderson and my d.o.b is four-dash-one-dash-twenty-zero-two …"

Mmh, I thought, a little surprised: she's only a year older, no, with a January birthdate, less than a year older than me. She was straight onto the next bit 'for the record' …

"My job title, specifically, is Commander, Marsbase One. My work here is the administration of this Mars base and the supervision of the work schedules of all of the staff here and those at other associated bases within easily communicable reach. At the moment that is just Mars Base Two."

Now Robin got down to the nitty-gritty.

"My first question - Ezra Pensak died in the airlock. What were you doing when this occurred and how did you become aware that something was wrong?"

"That is two questions, Robin."

My admiration for her went up. 'Good for you', I thought.

Robin was not programmed to be perturbed, however. "They are interrelated and therefore may be considered as one question," he explained patiently.

"I was checking over some diagrams which had been submitted by the surface workers based at Base Two. These related to rock and mineral strata. I carry in my mind a general awareness of where personnel are and the time function that goes with it. A warning came into my mind that Ezra should have returned by then. It didn't trigger in my mind any sort of alarm. No airlock system alarm had sounded. I simply put aside what I was doing and went to the airlock - I guessed that Ezra was doing a routine sand-cleaning task. The observation camera showed him lying stretched out. He wore no part of his space suit. The exit door was still open. I say 'still open' but it should not have been open at all with him not being in his suit."

"And then?"

"And then I rushed back to get Hans and we tried the door closer and the emergency override. Whichever worked, I'm not sure but one did. The exit door closed and air automatically bled into the centre chamber. Of course, we rushed in but it was soon clear to us that we were too late. Ezra was dead. My God, that was a sad moment. I'd never lost anyone before."

It seemed to me that Robin's next question revealed perfectly how AI does not carry with it what we humans call 'feelings'.

He said, "Was your 'sad moment' due to your feelings for the dead man, the human intelligence function which I do not compute, or, because you had 'never lost anyone before'?"

I felt like kicking him over. So much for my training! Even Rita blinked but Helen just answered …

"Due to my feelings."

Now Rita found, perhaps, the right words. "Human observer, Rita McKinley; input on last AI question …. Of course, you understand, Helen, that this is the sort of limitation that a non-human questioner places upon us - and why a human observer is required to be in attendance by UN law. Take it from me that David and I have the deepest sympathy for you and our feelings more than make up for Robin's lack of them. Of course, this is one reason why I wanted to push ahead and get it all done and dusted as they say, as quickly as possible. And that's why we should now push on, if that's OK?"

Helen stayed in control of her emotions and nodded.

"Carry on with your questioning, Robin," instructed Rita.

The robot had not moved at all. Now he came out of his imposed 'pause' state and resumed his programmed task.

"I would assume that you then removed the body. Did you immediately follow this with an examination of the airlock?"

"No; not immediately. I had a loose arrangement with the two operatives doing surface work that they could visit us and I communicated a warning to them to not come visit on that day as the airlock may not have been functioning properly. I had visions of another death - perhaps two."

"Why two? Isn't one, the one known as Alan Marsman, capable of breathing the Mars atmosphere?"

I thought of the depth of knowledge that must have been programmed into Robin. He seemed to know much more than I had thought he did. Someone on Earth, by that reckoning, knew quite a lot too. Meanwhile, Helen had a tricky little question to sort out and she wasn't rushing out her answer. After some thought …

"I guess I often don't think of Alan as a completely different creature, neither man nor Martian. And this is one of those moments: I just have a mental aberration and think of them as two men. Actually, to be correct, Alan does not have the capability to breath in the air on Mars in the sense of using it; he simply has a completely different metabolic system which makes breathing in *anything* irrelevant."

To me that seemed perfectly understandable but would the different sort of mind - if we can call it that - that Robin has accept that? He carried on as though he had.

"When you finally got around to the task of examining the airlock for a fault, did Hans take part in that procedure, whatever it was?"

"Yes, of course. As did Tan Lee."

"Why 'of course'? Hans is not qualified in electrics, electronics, or airlocks."

"None of us are. But we use it every day and our science degrees, not to mention our lab work, took in a lot of work with secure devices of a similar nature."

"You did not include Alan Marsman in your investigative team. Why not?"

"Well, although I know quite a lot about his scientific capabilities, I just didn't think that a person - creature if you like - who would not be affected by an airlock door open to the atmosphere would have the right mindset to spot the fault."

Mmmh, I thought. She's as good as Rita at leaving men out of things. Is there an increased feminism these days that I haven't heard about?

"In your report … your *accident* report … you seem to strongly suspect that it wasn't an accident. That it could have been a homicide. What led you to reach that conclusion?"

I guessed that this really put Helen on the spot. The case was taking on a complexity which could have really twisted her thinking at the time it happened. Maybe now she would have put a different code into the report. Also, what personal emotions were running through her thoughts at that time? Had she got any relationships, sexual or otherwise, which were playing with her mind then? Whatever the answer to these thoughts of mine, she was now the ice-lady. Her answer was delivered unemotionally ...

"That no alarms were triggered seemed very odd. Plus, I was aware of other tensions between members of our team. Obviously you will want to explore those. But, for me, that must be tomorrow. I have several other duties to perform and ... I'm whacked.

I wondered if Robin had been programmed for 'I'm whacked'.

....

Mars time 7.30 am, day 2. Place; again Helen's quarters.
Present; as on the previous evening.
Robin was ready for GO. He started by taking up where Helen had left off ....

"For the record: this questioning resumes where we closed previously. Helen Anderson, what did your subsequent investigation into a possible malfunction of the airlock door operation and what should have been an alarm response reveal?"

Helen nodded. She too was set for GO. "We - that is Hans and I - found that there is an electrical contact made through a copper contact strip. When a current is passed because the strip has been pressed onto an electrically positive current plate, a sound alarm is activated. This is a wailing sound audible throughout the base. Simultaneously a video picture of the central chamber is screened, visible to anyone in the main section of the base or near to the entrance door. Neither of these occurred. Hans and I both concluded that the contacts were in some way faulty and so no alarms or videos had been generated."

"Did you deduce a likely cause for this failure to have occurred?"

"Not conclusively but Hans suggested a possibility - that sand had somehow got onto the contact strip thereby reducing the electrical current passed to below the necessary voltage or amperage."

"Surely this electrical device is sealed against sand intrusion?"

"It is. And that was the main reason why I believed that the seal had been deliberately tampered with."

"For the record: your report has been passed on to technical experts at Hoyles. They are practised at investigating failures of their safety features. To date, their preliminary inquiry has not explained how a sand intrusion could occur given the standard sealing which their airlocks feature."

"Oh," was Helen's only response.

"Now, finally, to your other comments about 'tensions between members of the team' as you put it. Am I able to make deductions due to logical examination of these or, if these are symptomatic of human emotions, do conclusions need to be made by my human observer?"

"There may be certain relationships from which you may draw conclusions but, quite honestly as we humans say, deductions made from our answers - and some questions themselves - will require input and conclusions from humans as well. Mainly from humans, I should think. A sort of combined interrogation system, maybe."

"Agreed then. Would you please give your assessment of all the relationships and human feelings which you think we should consider in attempting to apportion blame or in reaching any other conclusion concerning the death of Ezra Pensak."

There was a long silence. I was immediately turning over in my mind how I would be able to contribute being that Rita had more-or-less banned me from taking part. She was probably considering now whether she could manage without some input from me - even if she were to control it. She must have known by now that I wasn't the most controllable person in the world; whatever world that was.

··········

The concluding part of Helen's testimony was about to begin. Would this be where I made my very first significant contribution. I had to smile inside my head: *What was I doing here?*

Robin began. "We had three humans on Mars when Ezra met his death. In addition, a part-human. Is that an acceptable definition?" Helen nodded. I made a mental note that it was useful to have an AI that could see and interpret physical movements such as a nod as well as speech and other verbal sounds. If it occurred, would he recognise from Helen the American sign with the single finger raised, I wondered.

"Would you please describe your assessment of their inter-relationships," Robin asked. This could be interesting, I thought.

Helen considered. "No-one likes another person in command. That is a burden one has to accept if you are in charge; in command. I always believed that if I was fair, even-handed, open with my subordinates, I would be tolerated, if not liked. If I could use my femininity with some of the men, that might give me an edge there. So, I have used it where I could. Of course, there is a converse to that if you have women subordinates - although I'm assuming traditional gender persuasions here, of course."

I guessed that, maybe Robin was out of his depth by now.

Helen went on. She didn't redden or seem ill at ease as she continued with her revelations ...
"The sexual act between humans doesn't necessarily, of course, demand loving feelings or anything else. Hans and I have indulged," she admitted. "Ezra, no. He was an extremely religious man. Jewish, of course. The main attraction for me, though, of Ezra was his diamond ring. Not his wealth. Just the ring."

"And where is that now?" I had to ask, thinking of Denton's comment at the briefing.

That drew a surprised look from Helen. I hadn't planned to make this my first contribution.

She said, in a slightly amused way, "It's where it has been for most of the time since he came here, in my safe under the bed there. You can see it when we finish."

"Why did you say, 'most of the time'?" I couldn't help asking.

"Ezra wore it only once - on his birthday, he said, but it was actually on some Jewish festival. Didn't they beat the Arabs once in a war?"

Now Robin pressed on with the remaining figures. "What about Tan Lee?" he asked first. "And, Alan Marsman?"

"I personally didn't find Tan Lee very attractive, although he could be quite interesting to talk to. He was quite into fossils and pre-history and had some convincing theories about Mars's past. As for Alan: you may have dismissed him from your thoughts altogether, let alone to do with relationships. He still retains many human features, however, though his voice is a bit weird. He has no lungs as we know them. Other organs to extract proteins and … well, I've never seen his physiology or had it explained. All I know is, he doesn't need or use the airlock."

"Oh," was all I could muster.

Rita had been quiet so far but now she got to the crux of the relationships questions. "You've told us how you and the others dovetail," she said. "But how do they fit with each other? Have you tagged any hatreds, jealousies, frustrations, whatever? Anyone threaten anyone else?"

"There were undercurrents: no outright falling outs. Ezra, as I've said, was very religious - he could soon be offended if anyone challenged his beliefs but I never witnessed him lose his temper over it and certainly not threaten anyone. Of course, I can't keep tabs on everything that's said. Hans is pretty laid back about most things - politics, religion, whatever. He would sometimes deliberately needle others but he did it gently and non-confrontationally. To him it would be a joke. Tan Lee? Mmmh. Tended to be neutral about most things. He was quite serious about his work - and good at it."

"How did he work with a non-human?" Rita asked.

"Oh, I think he barely noticed that. It was a working partnership and, since Alan was good at his job, that's what mattered most to Lee."

"Just to pick up on that last thing," I said. "Although not a relationship question: how, in what way, was Alan good at his job? Did being kind of Martian have, er, advantages?"

Helen nodded vigorously. "Too right it did. Getting about was one asset. He has got long, thin legs but big feet so, you should see him walk over sandy areas - and that's most places. Also, he has very nimble fingers although his hands are also big. Keen eyesight too. He can see very tiny things."

"Like grains of sand?" I asked.

"Oh, yes. And, if you haven't already noticed, Martian sand is almost microscopic."

I nodded and wondered if Rita had picked up on where I was going with this information.

It seemed a little strange for both Rita and Robin to round off the morning questioning session but Robin said in his usual emotionless tone, "For the record: I think that could conclude our questioning of Base Commander Helen Anderson. Of course, as with all witnesses, re-call for cross-examination or for new evidence to be presented is allowed. Next session; two-three-zero pm, today. Second witness, Hans Schroeder."

"Thanks everyone," added Rita. "Until then, do your own thing. David, if you want to suit up and join me, I'm going for a short stroll outside, before having some lunch."

A peace gesture, I wondered? But I was keen to go through the airlock again - and to 'get the feel' of actually standing on the red sands of Mars once more.

··········

We both trundled about outside but with little to say. We turned over rocks, although there weren't going to be any creepy-crawlies under them. I tried breaking a small piece off one but it was quite tough. I noticed that Rita did as I did at one time - picked up a handful of sand and let it trickle through her gloved fingers back down to the surface. I noticed how easily some stuck to my gloves although they were dry.

Eventually we'd both had enough - it was a pretty bland experience with no trees, grass with cows munching away, birdsong. No clouds too. Just a pale, butterscotch sky.

One thing we did do, something we'd ignored upon landing in our eagerness to get into the base: we walked over to the large United Nations flag, barely fluttering close to the base structure. I made my first comment then …

"Shouldn't we salute it," I asked with quirky humour. But Rita, whether seriously or not, said, "Definitely."

So, we raised our right arms in salute and I studied the design for the 20 seconds we honoured it. I went over in my mind what it was supposed to signify ….

The blue background I wasn't sure of but the white world map enclosed by twin laurel wreaths was all about worldwide peace. I'm not sure how I really felt at that moment. Back on Earth it would have been the usual cynical thoughts from me, but now - after the colossal journey here - and the obvious attempts to bring a system of law and cohesive order to the peoples on Earth or anywhere else we travelled to in the future - well! Quite thought-provoking. Mmmh! I didn't like having my normal equilibrium jolted.

I turned and joined Rita as we re-entered the base.

....

✿ ✿ ✿ ✿ ✿ ✿ ✿ ✿ ✿

Time: 2.30 pm, day 2. Place: Hans Schroeder's quarters.
Present: As before but with Hans there to be questioned instead of Helen.

Helen, having the privileges of rank, had bigger quarters than Hans so, we were a little more cramped but we followed a similar arrangement - Hans seated on his bed, Robin towering over him, and Rita and I seated on the same sort of collapsible, flimsy chairs as before.

"Ah!" sighed Hans. He looked quite relaxed and, as if to confirm this, he deliberately sprawled backwards on the bed propped by one arm. He made no attempt to out-stare Robin. Not many of us could do that.

As per the now assumed procedure, Robin gave the intro ...
"For the record; please confirm that you are Hans Schroeder and state your date of birth and job title. Would you then give us a brief summary of what work the job entails."

"Sure," said Hans but I noted that he pushed his free hand into his beard. Maybe this was a usual habit of his. He nodded also and began. "Yes, I am Hans Schroeder and my date of birth is the nineteenth of June, 1998. My job is 'Scientific Advisor, Martian Geology.' What that means is that I draw up maps and diagrams to show the underlying surface deposits, both minerals and water. It would include life forms too but we haven't found those - yet."

Robin's cold and undecipherable gaze bore down at Hans like a physical thing. A sword, perhaps.

"Why did you kill Ezra Pensak?" he asked.

I was staggered and Rita glanced up from her notepad to look at Robin almost like she was checking if he had malfunctioned. I cast my mind back to the techniques I recalled being used when AI began to be used in police interrogations and remembered; this was simply a shock tactic - and often used where a detainee is striving to be composed and relaxed. Certainly, Hans now sat back upright again.

"What is this?" he queried and there was an edge in his tone. "I don't know how you've jumped to that conclusion already. You haven't even asked me a single question yet." He paused, composing himself and deciding where to take this. However, as Helen had said, he was no fool and it came to him then - the disguised tactic; shock effect.

Robin merely carried on. "Did you discover the body?"

"No. Helen did. She will already have told you that."

"How did you then become involved?"

"I saw her walk out of the main section, the lounge, as we call it, towards the exit and the airlock. Maybe she was walking a little quicker than usual, I'm not sure, but it didn't seem particularly abnormal. No sign of panic and no warnings had been given. Then she was shouting for me urgently so I rushed out to her, schnell. She was looking through the observation window into the airlock and she turned to me looking absolutely stricken. It's Ezra, she said. I think he's had an accident. I looked and, somehow I knew

- he was tot. Dead. Then we messed about with the door controls and ..."

"Was the exit door open or closed?"

"It was clearly open but, as we hammered at various controls, it closed and everything began working normally again. When the indicator showed safe air pressure, our door, the entrance door, opened and we went in to the body, Ezra. But we both knew he was dead, although ..."

"Please, not *we*. You cannot speak for the Base Commander. *You* knew, or assumed, he was dead."

Hans looked annoyed at this correction. He said, sharply, "Helen reached him first and she said, 'He's dead.' Therefore, we *both* knew he was dead."

I thought, I bet Robin doesn't get corrected like that very often. However, he carried on ...

"And then? What did *you* do?"

Crumbs, I thought, an AI robot can hit back!

Hans shrugged. "Helen and I both tried a quick spell of chest compressions. She stood up to go fetch oxygen but I just shook my head: Hoffnungslose. So, we dragged him into the lounge and lifted him onto the table."

"For the human observer: How did you feel about this catastrophe?"

"I felt sick. That is how we humans feel sometimes."

"Even if you dislike the dead person: even hate him?"

"This was my second death - the previous one was on the Earth-moon and Helen can give you the record reference number for that - but I felt sick then. You see, I actually liked both victims."

"Did you kill the other one, too?"

Robin was remorseless, I thought.

Hans shook his head but I could see that it wasn't by way of an answer; it was in despair. Whatever the outcome would be, I felt sorry for the guy.

Rita stepped in and brought the second interrogation to a close.

....

Early evening saw the arrival of the last two to be questioned. Obviously Rita wanted to get it all finished on this, our day 2. Finish the questioning, that is. We might still be able to perform some rudimentary checks on the airlock door and the warning and safety systems during the following days. These examinations might show us the final clincher. Also, did she want some sort of discussion of the findings. A result. If it was decided a murder had been committed, what action would she take? What action *could* she take? Attempt to put a guilty party under restraint for months until our return flight could deliver him or her - or it - back to Earth? How was United Nations law to be applied on a Neutral Territory? I was pretty much confused. Was she?

We all ate a supper together but were very restrained and I for one had no appetite. Someone found a coin and that was the scientific tool we used to decide who'd be questioned next. Lee got the call right and went first which I was glad about: I figured he might be the quicker, less-taxing candidate. On this occasion the deceased subject of our efforts provided the quarters - he himself was resting under the Martian surface near to the UN flag.

As with Helen and Hans, while we settled ourselves, I glanced around at how Ezra had tried to enliven his quarters with photos and other personal items. There didn't seem to be anything which pointed to him being very wealthy and, searching for such items reminded me that we hadn't yet been shown the famous diamond ring.

Soon we had finished scuffling about and Robin took up his accustomed stance, towering over Lee. With Lee having a typical Chinese stature, the overwhelming difference in their body masses suggested a David and Goliath confrontation.

Robin came out with his usual starter …
"For the record: would you please confirm that you are Tan Lee and state your date of birth. Then, please state your job title and give a brief summary of the duties applying to this job."

Lee did this but with nervous little half-coughs. I'd always found it difficult to estimate a Chinese person's age and now I was surprised that he was the eldest of us on Mars. He was 55. Aside from his looks, he moved quickly and smoothly for an over-fifty. Perhaps he was into exercising or into some sporting activity. Maybe that 'sporting activity' was scrambling around on rock faces to get samples, I wondered.

Robin began …
"Are you content to be digging up the Martian surface in what is a fairly routine procedure or would you really prefer to be working back on the planet Earth?"

Lee hesitated then began to answer but, again, with his rather irritating cough. "I quite, ug, like it where I, ug, am now, thank you. This place …"

Rita broke in, "Would you like to have a beaker of cold water to sip while you give your answers, Lee? You seem to have something irritating your throat."

"Er, thank you. That might, ug, help. It's the Martian sand, you know." A full beaker was passed across to him and he took a quick drink spilling a few drops onto his tee-shirt.

I couldn't resist the obvious query - "But you would be working with your helmet on. Surely you don't get sand in that. If you do, I guess we're all going to be in trouble."

Rita explained. "Martian sand is so fine it can get everywhere. It beats most of our filters but, fortunately, in very microscopic amounts. Lee obviously has an extremely sensitive larynx. Probably worth you getting it checked out though, Lee," she added.

Robin worked out that he could now continue. Amazingly to me he had had a help system programmed into him. "You may answer 'yes' or 'no' to my following questions," he said. "Do you always work with Alan Marsman?"

"Er, yes."

"Do you ever go to the Main base alone?"

"Yes. But not often."

"Does he go there alone?"

"I don't, er, think so."

"If he did, could he go there without your knowledge?"

"Um, yes."

"Is that because you do not always work in close proximity to each other?"

"Yes. That is so."

"And he walks very quickly?"

"Um, yes, that is very true. He goes like a, um, train."

"Do you know who or what 'Sandman' is?"

"Yes. It's ..."

"Thank you, there is no need to explain." A slight pause from Robin, then, "Is it you who will benefit most by having this digging robot?"

"Er, yes. I suppose so."

"Because Alan Marsman, your colleague, is quite adept at digging into sand with his hands?"

"Yes, exactly. He has such big ..."

"OK, thank you. Do you *approve* of Alan Marsman?"

Here, Lee seemed to pause for some time before answering, "Approve? What do you, um, mean?"

"Approve in the sense that he is not human. Not entirely human, that is. It was intended by his creators that he function as a Martian. Do you agree with that intention? Yes or no?"

"I cannot, er, answer that with yes or no. There are, um, conditions. If I may ..."

"That is all, thank you, Tan Lee. I have finished my questions."

Lee didn't seem to accept that and I was in sympathy with him. He looked across at Rita with the appealing eyes of a chastised dog. She seemed at that moment to have an absorbing interest in the notes she had been writing. Unusually, perhaps; I decided to keep out of it.

· · · · · · · · · ·

Quicker and less taxing, I thought. Maybe not! Well, we were down to the last one now. Would we be questioning a Martian or just a one-off hybrid creature. A *thing* where no known parameters could be applied.

I couldn't wait, though, to see how he would tackle the mixed bag of searching questions, insults and pressures which would possibly be hurled at him. Well, to be fair though, we humans had tried to be considerate sometimes in our questioning. If Robin had been inconsiderate, well, he had all the limitations of a robot, with AI or not. It had been a fair interrogation so far, I thought. Not bad considering we had probably sat facing a murderer at some stage - or, was that still to come?

Ah, well! I might - just, might - find out at last what I was supposed to be doing here. Then I was hit by another thought - perhaps this last suspect, witness, interviewee, or whatever he was, had these same thoughts encroaching into his alien mind. Bring him on.

....

It was later into the Martian evening and, I knew, quite dark outside. We were passed the alcohol years - well, most people were. Most of us now accepted the special laboratory-concocted drugs which had the official stamp of approval (which were legal, in plain language) for when our brains needed a kicker. Even so, one of these tablets, taken with a rubbish drink, was a poor substitute for the old 'pint' or cocktail. Lee was making the best of it, though, by sitting alone at the lounge table and staring down moodily into his drink. He looked as though he'd passed on the pill.

When each of us felt ready we trooped one-by-one into Ezra's pad. Alan Marsman followed, glancing at Lee as he passed him. Lee kept his gaze down.

Where the previous, human objects of our questioning had been assessed as to their manner when they faced us, this was somehow more difficult with Alan. Was he relaxed or uptight in his posture or expression? Difficult to say. He was human in some respects but in other ways, though difficult to pin down just why, he wasn't. He went through different mannerisms expected of humans but with a strange twist. It was, I thought, like a man in evening suit who wears his jacket back-to-front and with the bow tie on his wrist. I realised that Robin would be lost on his assessment here and, from what I had heard when Alan had said something in the background, with tonal judgement too. Was this my chance to come into the picture, I wondered, with a degree of cynicism.

However odd, we somehow had to make some sense of the way he handled his questioning. This final session began in the now familiar way …

"For the record," droned Robin. "Please confirm that you are named Alan Marsman. Then, give us your job title and what you do in that job."

No date of birth, of course.

"I do confirm that I am Alan Marsman," he said, with the strange mixed frequencies of speech that we had all heard a little of but to which we new arrivals still had to adjust. "My job title is Assistant, Martian Geology Exploration. I believe that title in itself tells what I am expected to do."

I smiled inwardly. Another awkward bugger, I thought. Two of us!

"Do you assist Tan Lee in his work?" continued Robin, not at all put out by the first answer.

"Yes."

"Does part of those duties require that you visit Mainbase quite frequently?"

"Yes."

I wondered if one of his implanted qualities had been to save energy!

"And were those visits usually made by you alone?"

"Yes."

"Why was that?"

"Because they were mostly to take records or notes compiled by Tan Lee."

"Thus saving him a journey?"

"Yes."

"Because you were quicker?"

"Yes."

"Or, because you had your own reasons for the visits?"

"Yes, sometimes."

"And what reasons did you have on those 'sometimes'?"

"I wanted to converse with Ezra."

This shook both Rita and me. We needed time to consider before the question train rumbled on. However, Robin didn't wait for us humans or slacken his theme …

"Converse about what?"

"God."

Again, Rita and I were shaken. Proof of that was when she locked her widened eyes onto mine. I fully expected her to intervene but she didn't. Maybe, too shocked. And I didn't because I had to know where this would lead and Robin seemed to be on the right train-track for us to find out. Thinking dispassionately, nothing had yet really been said: it was just that totally unexpected answers had been given - and given in an open, slightly challenging way.

Robin carried on. "Would you please elaborate as to why you chose to converse about a subject which does not appear to be associated with your work duties? By 'your' I mean 'your singular' not 'your as a pair'."

Alan wasn't into nodding or grunting: he just continued as smoothly and unconcerned as with his previous answers …

"I was responding to a particular remark he had made on a previous visit and follow-up remarks he had then made during my subsequent visits."

"Please give a brief summary of the gist of the various remarks made by Ezra which you seem compelled to have had to respond to."

Again, no nod. "Ezra said to me during one of my early visits, 'Were you indoctrinated in a belief in God?' I said that I had been given information about the concept of there being an almighty being but that this concept varied among different peoples. I explained in a little more depth but what I said was simply the accepted teaching at non-faith schools He must already have been aware of this accepted practise."

"Except that he was almost surely taught at a faith school," interjected Rita.

"Even so," I contributed my two-pennyworth, "He was perhaps curious as to just which religion or version of that religion was being taught to …" I hesitated to name the species which had been man-made. Strange, I thought, but no-one seemed to have openly come out with an official name for this man-created species. Ah, how careful people can be not to upset another's feelings, came the cynical thought.

Robin again got us on track. My thought was, it isn't in an AI robot's programming to try to pursue arguments or get involved in religion and its many gods. However, he just asked, "Briefly, if you please: How did the period of conversations on this topic conclude?"

For the first time, even Alan was forced to pause. Then, the answer which stunned us all …

"Ezra said to me, 'You are an abomination. You are not one of God's creatures. You must; yes, you must die!'

When I had got my breath back and my scrambled mind was getting back some cohesion, I found I was the first to say anything. I became a Robin substitute …

"So, how did you react to this? It must have …"

"My education and training left me with only one course of action. I planned and carried out the murder of Ezra Pensak. This was in accord with my safety reactions guidance program."

Once more, Rita was aghast - and silent. I was aware that both of her hands were clutching the side-frame of her chair with a force which might have crushed it. Robin - perhaps in accord with his programming - (job done?) - went into 'standby' mode. I didn't try to crush my chair or go into 'standby'. Later I felt rather proud that I reacted at all - and not too badly either. First, I gave Alan my coldest stare,

"Alan, stay just where you are. The base commander needs to be made aware of what you've just said so, I'm leaving right now to fetch her," and I repeated firmly, "Stay just where you are."

··········

✧ ✧ ✧ ✧ ✧ ✧ ✧ ✧ ✧ ✧

I was to find out in the next few days what a messy, uncertain calamity had struck our little community on Mars. In my simple, normally quite-organised mind, there could have been fewer factors to add which could have made it worse. I'll run through those we had already to show what a picture - a horrific, chaotic picture - we all faced. All except Alan Marsman, self-confessed murderer, that is. I'll get to him shortly.

Just to skip what happened late on day 2, after we (this became everyone on the base, of course) had had everything revealed, consider our circumstances ....

1. We had no-one with absolute authority. Rita and Helen still shared that in a bizarre way.

2. We, they, had no regulatory body present. No police force. We all were the police.

3. To communicate our circumstances to Earth by radio was no problem but for this to initiate a visit by a relief vessel would take months.

4. Until relief arrived we faced the day-to-day task of getting organized and jobs done.

5. What to do with our murderer. We had no jail even if that could be considered, but, if it wasn't, then ...

6. What about our safety. Murderers sometimes get a taste for it!

Things got a little more sorted when we did the sensible thing - we held a meeting with all present. Because we were all tired and confused and needed some thinking time, we decided it would not be that same evening but that it would be held the next morning, day 3, in the lounge.

We reluctantly had to put onto one side any possible threat from Alan. No-one was going to volunteer to give up sleep to keep him under surveillance.

....

The start of day 3 began reasonably enough. We were all refreshed by sleep and then by our limited ablutions routines (God, I missed a hot shower). Then, soon enough, we were eating and starting to chat. Another freshening up and we slowly gathered in the brightly-lit lounge to see what we should see.

One of the consequential results of us all being thrown together was that two subtle pairing-offs began to take place - Rick and Rita and, yes, you've guessed right, me and Helen. Where this would go may have been uncertain but, with months to go - well one can have high hopes. However, there was no other simple friendship formed. Hans and Lee didn't seem to bond and, well, Alan was an outcast for now. Of course, things could change in the long days to come.

It needed someone to prod us into assuming some degree of being organised and that was, perhaps appropriately, the base commander. Helen had no bell to ring or glass to strike so she simply clapped her hands forcibly together. We all looked towards her and the slight chatter died a death. The only person still standing sat down and we were ready for GO.

Helen spoke, gently but firmly. "Good morning to you all. I'm sure you would all agree that one of our priorities, perhaps the prime one - can you have a 'prime priority?" I knew that she had tried to inject slight humour to get us to relax but that humour might be in short supply in the following days. "Anyway, we need to set up an agreed command structure on this base for, until a relief ship arrives from Earth in maybe 4 months' time, we have some serious decisions to make. I do not believe we can work properly with a dual command system so my first proposal is that Rita McKinley be given complete authority to command this base and all the personnel on it. This must include, of course, our contacts with Earth and any vessels they may send to land here. If anyone does not agree with my choice for Base Commander will they speak up and give us their reasons."

I spoke but it wasn't to disagree. "I am agreeing with your choice," I clarified, "But, can we assume that base 2 is now to be closed down so, Marsbase One will be the only operational base remaining on Mars?"

Helen nodded. "I have assumed - but it is for the new base commander to decide - that base 2 be used for storage only. OK?"

I nodded and she continued. "Anyone else have anything to say or can we hand over to our new Base Commander, Rita McKinley?" she smiled as she waved a hand at Rita.

It seemed settled but then, to general consternation, a long arm was raised. It belonged to Alan, our admitted murderer.

Helen said very coldly, "Alan?"

The odd, squeaky voice rose. "I'm not querying the general vote which seems to be for Rita … On a technicality, will the new Base Commander be applying Earth's United Nations law here? I've heard she is an authority on it."

The low hub-hub raised a notch.

Rita now pushed her way through to a position where she could see everybody and they could see her. Her face looked like that of a commander - tight but firm; her lips pressed together and her eyes searching about but then locking Alan's.

"It could be difficult to have to invent our own law system. We don't want endless meetings and arguments so, yes, Alan, as I have been trained in UN inter-state laws, I shall use them - apply them – rigorously."

Alan was not satisfied. His voice dropped a notch now he had her attention but he pursued his point. "But, aren't many of the inter-state laws still being formulated: some still being drafted, amended even? Particularly those concerning Neutral Territories - and others concerning AI robotics?"

Rita, despite her extensive grasp of UN inter-state laws, must have been extremely annoyed at this early intervention. She hid it well but, I guessed, knowing that she was being pushed on this sticky issue by a self-confessed murderer, she was already seeking in the back of her mind where he was going with it and any possible consequences from that. She had to wrap it up ….

"I shall use my knowledge of the laws as they exist and use them as a bed-rock. Where there is doubt as to their proper interpretation, I have been given the authority by this meeting today to make my own judgement as to the best application in each case as I see it. I can only affirm that I shall be fair and unbiased in making my decisions relating to recommended UN procedures."

A pretty good attempt to shut Alan up, I thought, and, for now, it seemed to work.

She drew in a deep breath and got down to procedures ...

"I shall not run this base with the help of a committee - only because I have always found committees unwieldy to say the least. However, it is not my intention to shut anyone out. I shall quickly turn for advice to anyone who has specialist knowledge and they will help me in my decision making. Now - some of you - those with specific jobs and who have contracts with the UN or one of its approved contractors, will know when their return dates are. For your information, my own contract is open-ended. I was sent here to see this business of Ezra Pensak's death through to a conclusion. That conclusion has apparently been reached by Alan's open confession. However, resulting action from that still has to be decided."

"By whom?" came the now familiar squeaky voice.

"By me, Alan. By me alone. But, as I've already stated, I will make my judgement based on UN inter-state law."

Alan was like the proverbial animal that will not let go. This first meeting, which I had hoped would go so well, was already developing into a duel between the new Base Commander and the new self-confessed murderer. I was prepared to sit back and see how it went: who would win. But, at the same time, I was getting anxious. I knew what outcome I wished for but it was already too soon to put money on it happening.

"So, if I may be the first to have my future decided, what do you plan for me?"

He was certainly putting Rita with her back to the wall. I guessed she hadn't wanted his unique circumstances to be decided upon and acted upon so soon - and in front of us all. If I had been in her shoes, my choice would have been to retire to the privacy of my own office but with some advisor who I could trust to point me in the right direction. Maybe Rick, came to mind. However, none of that was to be …

"My plan for you, Alan, is that you will leave on the next return flight to Earth. You would then …"

"Ah, no!" The squeaky voice was raised two notches. "I too was sent here, not with a contract, maybe, but with an open-ended *understanding*. This was by the UN's Scientific Experimental Procedures Department. I don't believe your previous experience or work has been with them. I shall be staying here indefinitely."

I wondered if there was such a UN department. Rita spent a quick minute trying to place it also - and deciding where her powers lay. Could she send him back to Earth? Of course, radio contact with Earth was quick - an 8-minute daily slot which then whizzed a communication via the Mars orbiter to mother Earth in as little as 4 minutes but was probably now up to 10 minutes. Daily, though. But getting it through the giant United Nation's messy inter-department systems would stretch it out from maybe one day to several days. And, if it ever arrived at the right desk, how long to be dealt with? Oh dear, I groaned to myself: forever!"

Rita frowned. "I shall have to consult on that one." A typical administrator's stalling tactic, I thought. "And what about your food and quartering?" she asked Alan.

"Duties of a base commander," he replied. "Responsible for all personnel on the base. And, I shall come and go as I please." It wasn't a question but Rita answered it.

"Yes, provided you do not interfere with the duties of other personnel on the base - and subject to any instruction I may receive from the UN."

That seemed to wrap up Alan's particular case.

I wasn't happy. Perhaps it was because I had detected a distinctly human-like characteristic in Alan which I had not before come across - smugness. Yes, I'd always been averse to anyone being smug with me and here we had a self-confessed murderer being smug with us all. It didn't sit right with me but it looked as though I was going to have to live with it. I'd found before that I could never shut out of my mind frustrations like this. I knew I would be turning them over in my mind constantly even if they were unresolvable: and this one was looking unresolvable.

Eventually the meeting reached its conclusion. I had learnt that Helen, Hans and Lee would be returning to Earth with me. Hans had applied for an extension of his time on Mars but that was before Ezra's death. He hadn't made up his mind yet whether to let that ride.

We dispersed but I caught up with Rita and said "Can I have a word, Rita?"

"It'll have to wait until after lunch. What's it about? Anything urgent?"

"I'm not sure it's urgent but I just want a chat, maybe half-an-hour, to clarify some things."

"I can guess what," she said dryly. "OK, then - how about 2.30?"

"Yep, that'll do fine."

"Just you and me?"

I nodded. "Yes. See you then."

She gave a return nod and went to her new office. Hans followed her and I assumed he'd already booked a session to discuss whether or not he should apply for an extension to his time on Mars. Lee looked rather forlorn and sat with a drink staring at a crossword in front of him but not seeming quite with it.

Helen sat with Rick and, although I could feel a toilet session coming on, I said, "Mind if I join you?" Helen waved a hand at a spare seat next to her.

"Alan the murderer has gone outside; walkies." She said, "So Rick and I were talking about it. What a messy situation."

"He doesn't seem bothered by it," Rick said. "Glad I've not got to sort it out."

"You might be given the privileged position of chief advisor," I grinned.

Rick pulled a face, "Chief executioner, would suit me better," he said.

"Rick! Are you a death penalty advocate?" asked Helen, looking surprised.

"Fundamentally, maybe not. Trouble is, finding a good alternative. There's arguments for and against - and some good points in those arguments but, at the end of the day, to use a good old Earth expression, I always seem to find myself falling back on one indisputable fact - if a murderer is executed, well, he ain't going to do it again. Behind bars forever would be my second choice but 'forever' is never guaranteed."

"I'd joined you to see what views you'd got on Alan," I said. "It seems you have both been chewing it over and ..." I looked from Helen to Rick and back again, ..."at least one of you has a pretty firm opinion."

Helen sighed gently, "I'm firm - but it's the other way."

I stood up, maybe I had got something from this but I would think it over during the lunch period.

"Nature calls," I told them and strolled away to my quarters.

....

I hadn't worked out exactly what to say but I knew it would come once we started talking. Rita waved me into the chair in front of the desk and I lowered myself into it. I did my usual glance around. Mostly the room was still littered with Helen's stuff. I wasn't sure about the framed photo of a handsome young man in a US marines uniform but, with Helen being American, I guessed he was her son unless, of course, she was a 'cradle-snatcher'.

"If you've finished your look around, let's get started," hustled Rita. "I'm betting this is all about what we do with Alan."

"Ah-huh!" I confirmed. "In particular and more accurately, what is the UN going to do with him?"

Rita leaned back and stretched her shapely body at the same time. "You probably aren't the only one here who is trying to figure out what should be done: what can be done. We're in unchartered territory here, as they say. I've said we must be bound by UN law. But that law is still being worked out by the bureaucrats back home. At least, the finer points of it are - together with the complex areas like, what law do we impose in Neutral Territories."

"Yeah, it's a mess," I said. "But what I would like to know, and I expect the others would as well, is how are *you* going to apply it here on Mars?"

Rita put on her tough, commander's look. "Law with a capital L is never easy to frame. I think a good example of how it can seem quite shitty to ordinary men in the street, to use a well-used British expression - ordinary citizens, if you like - is where we have - and we have had - young kids who have committed heinous crimes, even, technically, murder. What punishment or correction should be applied to, say, a ten-year-old killer? I've known kids of that age who I believe are totally evil. They know what they are doing as well as some older people do. But we - law with a capital L - sets a different condition for the two cases."

I nodded. "I can see where we're going with this."

"Then you can see that Alan, in a way, is like the kid…"

"But, he's extremely intelligent. He's like an ordinary human. I wouldn't give him special consideration."

"You wouldn't but the United Nations will - does. And why? Because he isn't even classed as a human being. Would you charge an ape with murder? Alan's DNA as well as his body has been, what? Chopped about, changed. How can we judge him?"

I thought about it. "Well, the UN, having created this non-human, then proceeded to give it human rights and privileges. They gave it a job, no different from that of a fellow worker. Gave it a home and food. There are thousands of people back on Earth who would give anything for the chance to get to Mars. He got it. If he lives to be 50 he'll probably finish up as Base Commander." I paused for a breath then continued, "So - being given rights and privileges comes with having responsibilities. He seems to have chucked those away."

Rita sat up and leaned forward. "There's a second reason for special treatment." I guessed what this would be but eased myself back in my seat. Rita was a good advocate I had to admit. She proceeded ...

"Neutral Territories. The UN has had a bellyful of disputes concerning those back on Earth - and also with respect to the Moon. Now the United Nations is becoming, believe it or not, very much more united as a body; more and more of its members are realising that we need good, solid inter-state law. We need that to prevent wars breaking out." She smiled. "The new slogan is, if you want to practice it - 'law not war'."

"What, even China has agreed?" I couldn't resist.

"Yes; even China."

"So - how does this hit us on Mars? Where does Alan fit into this global-now-interplanetary law system? Is it his trial - or his punishment?"

Rita smiled. "To start, Alan is stateless. No universal system for conducting trials has yet been agreed - the differences among the nations is too great but, it is being sorted ..."

I shook my head slowly and sadly from side-to-side. "I'll bet it is. Over banquets and wine."

Rita ignored - or appeared to do so - my sarcasm. She ploughed on ...

"And then, to come, will be the agreed, er, consequences; punishment if that fits."

"Let me sum this up if I may," I said with assumed weary resignation. "Alan gets off scot free."

She waited for more but that was the total of my summing up. Her follow up did the real summing up ...

" 'Fraid so, David."

The subject was now closed but as I stood up to leave she said, "Robin. He's standing all forlorn in the airlock. Switched off. It's OK for him to stay where he is until he goes back to Earth for re-programming or whatever role he has to play but - I assume his batteries will require re-charging sometime so that he can make his own way onto the ship. No hurry, of course: that won't be for a month or so. Here's his controller" - she handed me the complicated-looking device but we had similar ones at Intel-Robotics. I shoved it into my wasteband and trudged out of her office.

....

Rick was trying to give Lee a lift by helping him with his crossword. Helen was reading something. Hans was nowhere to be seen. I wasn't really in the mood now for discussing anything with anybody. I decided to examine Robin, mainly to make sure that when I got around to re-charging his batteries I would know how. Most AI robots were now following a similar style of construction, the only major difference between Robin and ours at Intel-Robotics was that ours were wheeled; Robin was two-legged. This meant a slight difference in the controller, of course, but nothing I couldn't figure out. I guessed I might have to move him if he wasn't already near to a charging point.

I checked out the airlock and it was on safe-mode. I remembered that Alan was out somewhere but so? He couldn't just enter it while someone was in there - at least, assuming the safety systems were now still working faultlessly. Never-the-less, I hesitated for a fraction before pushing the 'Open' button and entering. I strolled in and looked over towards the corner where Robin stood quite immobile. Then I froze in shock - half hidden by the robot's huge bulk was the gangly figure of Alan.

He just stood there, quite motionless and obviously awaiting my reaction and my comment.

"Oh! What are you up to, Alan?" I queried.

He took a single step away from the robot. "I could ask you the same question. Robin's in standby, so?"

I was annoyed that this creature which I had a growing dislike for was questioning me. But I had to say something.

"He'll need re-charging," I explained with assumed patience. "My job. Although I won't be doing it for some time, I thought I'd refresh my memory about this type. It's put together slightly differently from those I'm familiar with so I need to check where the batteries are, how you get at them and - where the power point is and is it within reach. There! That's me. What about you?"

I'd given him a longer explanation than I wanted to but at least I'd smashed the ball back into his court.

"Thought I'd do some familiarisation too."

"But, he's not your responsibility," I said firmly. I didn't want him mucking about with Robin.

"Not my responsibility maybe, but I've got a special interest in him."

I couldn't see it. "Oh, and what's that?" I pursued.

I was then completely taken aback by the venom he put into his next words …

"Because this is the mother who tried to get me convicted with his questions," he spat out. I guessed the American-style blasphemy was learned during his training spell in Arizona.

"He was only following a programmed routine," I explained but I guessed he already knew that. "Everyone got the same treatment." There was a pause. I was still facing him, rooted to the spot where I had first seen him. He remained close by the robot from when he'd stepped into view. "So - what good will your 'special interest' achieve?" I wasn't sure but a suspicion was beginning to grow.

"What I *feel* like doing is kicking the mother's head in. What I can do is tear its effing guts out - when you've shown me where the batteries are."

"Sounds crazy," I said. "But if that's what you want - it won't bother me. Now ..." I withdrew the controller from my pants, studied it and clicked a button. Robin's eyes blinked, the signal that he was no longer on standby. "There," I said. "Now we can see where his batteries are."

Alan started to move out a little further so that he could see what was what - but that wasn't at all in my plan. I pressed another button ....

Robin moved, a little clumsily but with enough speed. He trapped Alan between his massive leg and torso and the corner walls of the airlock. I had put my bet on his 550 pounds of metal alloys being far too unstoppable by the much lighter though well-built Alan. A squeaky groan was emitted then silence from the man-made creature. He would never murder again. Even the scientist-surgeons who had created him would not be able to mend him. I couldn't tell immediately but my guess, that of a crushed skull, was quite accurate. What now? I wondered.

....

What now and a little while later was, the body was removed and everyone was advised of what had happened and that there would be a meeting at 6.30 pm.

I was surprised a little but Rita chose to get Alan buried before it got dark, so we tried out Sandman and, with a little help from Rick and Hans, a second mound was created under the UN flag.

Rita then summoned me into her office. I knew that whatever the later meeting would decide, my future was in her hands.

She did a fake groan as I plonked myself down in the same chair I'd sat in before.

"Good heavens, Dave! Did this have to happen? What went on in there? Tell me it was an accident."

"No, it wasn't an accident, Rita. The truth has to be told - it was murder. Another case of …."

She shook her short, blond locks in despair. "Stop! Why did you have to go to these lengths just to satisfy your idea of what justice should be?"

I'd let her go on. Now I shook my head vigorously. "Wait a minute, Rita. You just said, 'why did you'. It wasn't me. Forget ideas of justice. Forget neutral territories as well if you like. *Robin* killed Alan. *Deliberately and in self-defence.* The question is, though, Rita; when you start applying your United Nations law - with a capital L - will Robin, an artificial intelligence robot, be found guilty?"

The End

Other books by Trevor Palmer

Non-fiction: **The Young Giants** – a comparison of the early years of Albert Einstein and Sir Isaac Newton.
Chess for Ordinary Mortals
Looking back on 6 months with Ryan

Fiction: **The Ant Gods** – action drama in the world of ants.
Funny Worlds – sci-fi humorous shorts
The Grand Tour of Funny Worlds; Light Years from the Truth and **The Pharaoh, The Writer ... and the Last Green Bottle** – a trilogy of sci-fi adventure and intrigue featuring Dave Hogarth.
From Beyond the Blue Planet – sci-fi
The Final Mind-leap – sci-fi

Fiction for teenagers: **Dobbo's most boring holiday,** sci-fi

Made in the USA
Middletown, DE
23 July 2018